Conrath

House of ROYALS

INTERNATIONAL BESTSELLING AUTHOR
KEARY TAYLOR

ALSO BY KEARY TAYLOR

FALL OF ANGELS

Branded

Forsaken

Vindicated

Afterlife: the Novelette Companion to Vindicated

THE EDEN TRILOGY

The Bane

The Human

The Eve

The Raid (an Eden Short Story)

The Ashes (an Eden Prequel)

THE McCAIN SAGA

Ever After Drake

Moments of Julian

Depths of Lake

Playing it Kale

WHAT I DIDN'T SAY

In the world of vampires, families are not always born of blood, they are earned through blood…

House of
ROYALS

Prologue

FALLING FOR THE MAN WHO would one day be my worst enemy was the most dangerous thing I could have done—and I was constantly surrounded by people who wished to kill me. He made me vulnerable. My feelings for him left me exposed to those who would manipulate and take advantage of me.

Opening my heart to him meant opening the door to losing myself.

I thought I was a good person. I thought I knew right from wrong.

But in this world of secrets and lies and blood, all the lines have blurred. All the circumstances leading to this means to the end are gray.

And I'm not sure who I have become.

One

A GIANT SET OF ORNATE gates is the first glimpse I'm offered of the Conrath Estate. Ornately sculpted iron twists and curls and frames the beautiful relief sculpture of a raven in the middle of a crest. The line down the middle where the two gates come together is barely even visible. They're anchored by two great stone pillars, which connect to the giant iron fence that seems to imprison the whole property.

"Think I just ring the button there?" the driver asks with uncertainty.

"I guess," I offer, just as tentative as him. I peer through the gate, but all I can see is rolling green property and a well-kept gravel driveway.

The driver presses the button. I expect to hear a voice, demanding to know what we want. But instead, there is simply a buzzing sound and the gates swing open.

There must be hundreds of trees lining the driveway. Sprawling green lawns stretch beyond, rolling into gardens and unknown places. I catch sight of a barn, a guest house, a garage. A house starts to crest into view. The driveway circles into a giant loop with a water feature at the center, framed with well-trimmed, perfectly solid green hedges. There are flowers spilling everywhere, beautiful stonework creating garden edges, sculptures of gargoyles, angels, and dark creatures that hide in the beauty of it all.

But none of that can hold my attention.

Not when there's that house before me.

Or rather, mansion.

What looks to be the original house is tall and grand. Two stories with a massive porch supported by eight gigantic white pillars. Mantles decorate the space above each window. It's perfectly white, the paint flawless despite the obvious age of the house.

Extending from either side of the house are two massive wings, one to the north, one to the south. They're stone, ancient, and perfect looking at the same time.

The place is massive. Like a Southern, antebellum castle.

My heart picks up double time, taking up residence in my throat.

I've had a week to anticipate my arrival. But the reality of actually being here is overwhelming.

I climb out from the backseat and the driver pops the trunk to remove my two suitcases, setting them in the gravel. He stands there expectantly, and it takes me a beat too long to realize that I still need to pay him. I dig in my purse and hand him the cash.

"Good luck, miss," he says in his heavily Southern accent. He tips his hat to me, climbs back in the cab, and starts back down the driveway. The taxi's tires grind through the gravel as it pulls away.

My driver gets to go back to his normal life, while I am left here with only the unknown. I watch him go and go until the car is out of sight, pulled down the long drive and around the bend. Because once he's gone, I have to accept that I'm here and I'm not leaving.

I take a quivering breath and turn to face the house.

Mansion.

It sits on, I don't even know how many, acres of pristine landscape. And there's the Mississippi river directly behind it. Some kind of insect chirps around me, one I don't know the name of yet because I don't know anything at all about Mississippi other than that the river is named after it.

But it is my home now. I guess.

I grab my two suitcases, everything I own that is of worth in them, and finish the walk up the driveway to the doors.

"Good afternoon, Miss Ryan."

Suddenly, my heart is in my throat and my foot slips on one of the steps. The man who had opened the door takes a step toward me.

"My apologies, I didn't mean to startle you," he says, blinking slow and hard. He reaches forward and offers a hand.

"It's fine," I stutter, setting one of the suitcases down so I can accept his handshake. "I just forgot that you were going to be here."

"May I help you with your bags?" he offers.

"Uh, sure," I say uncomfortably, indicating for him to take the one on the porch. He grabs it and turns back into the house.

He walks in, easy as day and night, like his surroundings are no big deal. But the second I step foot inside, I freeze in awkwardness.

Because standing just inside is a row of people.

"Welcome, Miss Ryan," a few of them mutter.

But the greeting is cold and uncomfortable.

Because when they say it, not a one of them looks me in the eye.

"Miss Ryan," the man who greeted me says. "This is the staff. Katina, the house cook," he says, indicating a plump woman with brilliant red hair. "Angelica and Beth, the housekeepers. Juan, Dave, and Antonio, our grounds men. And Kellog, our handyman."

I struggle for words. I wasn't expecting any of them. "Uh, hello."

Still none of them look at me. The man beside me gives a nod and they disburse without a word.

The breath leaks between my lips slow and heavy now that they aren't all standing here. And finally my eyes are free to take in the scene before me.

With absolute wonder.

The entryway is grand and spacious. A double staircase splits at the bottom and reconnects at the top of the next floor. A giant, crystal chandelier hangs from the ceiling. High windows let in the late afternoon sunlight. Paintings hang from the walls. The marble floor shines with a high luster. Crown molding, gold leafing, and sculpted detail are thrown everywhere around me.

Saying the place is beautiful would be an understatement. This house is grand, ornate, and way too rich for my blood.

And somehow, it's all mine.

"Miss Ryan?" the man calls from down the hall. I didn't even realize he'd walked away. "After we drop your bags off, I can show you around, if you'd like."

"Okay," I answer breathily. With one last look around, I follow him down the hall that branches off to our right.

More paintings line the dark hallway, illuminated dimly with smaller versions of the chandelier in the entryway. Down four doors we go before the man opens one and we step in.

"This is only a guest bedroom, but until you decide which room you'd like to claim as yours permanently, I thought you'd be comfortable here."

"Thank you," I say, setting my suitcase next to its sister on the floor. "I'm sorry, remind me of your name again?"

"Rath," he says as I meet his eyes. They're dark, possibly even black, except when the light catches them just right. He's certainly some kind of African-American, but I'd guess he had a mix of something else in his DNA, too. Native American, maybe? Small lines next to his eyes make me wonder how old he is. Late thirties?

Early forties? Neatly trimmed, curly hair hugs his head. He's strong, fit, and looks ready for anything.

"Rath," I repeat, recalling the name from the will. Silently, I wonder about this man having the condensed version of my father's last name as his *only* claimed name. But it would be rude to ask about that.

"It's nice to meet you," he says, when I show my lack of intelligent conversation.

"You, too," I recover. "I'm sorry. This has all just been such a whirlwind and I'm feeling a little…"

"It's perfectly all right if you're feeling overwhelmed," Rath says as we exit the guest bedroom and walk back out into the hall. "You're going through a drastic life change. You've moved over a thousand miles from your home. Trust me, where you've just come from is a completely different world from which you've arrived."

It's true. Everything here is different. The landscape. The feel of the air. The way people talk. Everything.

"So," Rath says as we walk back into the grand entry room. "A little bit of history on the house. It was built in 1799, making it the forth oldest home still standing in Silent Bend. The man who built it emigrated from England. He and his brother both bought mass amounts of land and established cotton plantations. The Estate continued as a plantation for 86 years, but was then shut down and landscaped and eventually transformed into what it is today."

Rath walks back into the grand entryway and stops under the chandelier. "It was brought here from Bohemia," he says as he looks up at it. Light dances off its surface, casting rainbows and shoots of brilliance in all directions. "The thing is nearly four hundred years old and priceless. Despite all the grandeur you see around you, this is the heart and crown of the Estate."

"It's beautiful," I say as I look up at it. And it is. I realize as I look closer that it doesn't have any light fixtures inside, it is simply the way the light comes through the windows that makes it appear to be glowing.

"The staircases themselves took the carpenters and welders ten months to construct," Rath continues. They are indeed ornate and beautiful. The iron twists and curls, much like the gates leading into the property. Flowers, thorns, and tiny ravens are woven throughout the masterpiece. "Here on the main floor there are eight bedrooms, seven bathrooms. Upstairs there are six bedrooms, nine bathrooms, and the master suite. You are, of course, welcome to claim any you choose."

Last week I had one bedroom I could barely squeeze a queen-sized bed and a dresser into. Now I have more than a dozen of them to choose from.

We walk back through the grand entrance and enter an enormous ballroom. It can't be anything else. Polished marble floors show me my reflection. Chandeliers hang from the ceiling. Massive drapes hang to the sides of the cathedral-shaped windows. And that view outside? Breathtaking. The gardens. The pool. The river. But what dominates the room is the giant raven crest inlaid in the center of the floor.

"I don't think this room requires too much explanation," Rath says with a small smile.

I imagine the gowns that must have twirled here once upon a time, the kisses that must have been shared, the laughter and the music that must have filled this space.

And it all feels alien to me.

"You know, I think most girls dream of what it would be like to be a princess, to never have to worry about money again. To learn they have this grand life that was always awaiting them," I say as I take it all in, turning slowly as I do. "But the reality of it is...well. I don't have words for it. I don't think it's going to feel real for a very long time."

Rath gives me a look. Sadness. Respect. Weight. And I think there's meaning behind it all, but I don't quite understand it. "Come," he says finally, turning and exiting the ballroom.

We don't go far. Off from the ballroom, he shows me a small, informal dining room, and just behind it is a grand, master chef kitchen. It takes my breath away.

"Do you like to cook?" Rath asks as I marvel over it.

"I bake," I say, tracing my fingers over the beautiful stainless steel ovens. "I don't cook much else, but I've worked at a bakery for the past four years."

"Well, we do have the house cook," Rath explains further.

"Katina," I say, forcing myself to commit the names of the staff to memory.

Rath crosses his hands behind his back and looks regal doing it. "Of course, you don't have to keep her, but she is the best in Mississippi."

"I don't feel right firing anyone," I say with a small smile and a chuckle. "If they like their job, they can keep it. It's not my money that's paying their salaries."

"But it is your money," Rath says with a half-smile and a raise of one of his eyebrows.

"I suppose so," I say uncomfortably, tucking a lock of hair behind my ear.

"Would you like to see your vehicles?" he offers when he sees how uncomfortable I am.

He opens a door that lets into a massive garage.

Sitting inside are four shining, beautiful vehicles. A lightning quick-looking black Ferrari, a black and silver motorcycle, a rugged-looking red Jeep, and a classic baby-blue Porsche.

"I can't drive any of those," I say with a strangled sounding laugh. "They all look like they'll break the second I breathe on them." Last week I was driving a twenty-year-old beater that smelled like exhaust all the time. On the inside.

8

"I'm sure you'll be fine," Rath says with a smile.

I let out a heavy breath as he shuts the door, and I follow him through the ballroom again out onto the veranda out the back.

"The grounds crew work fulltime. The three of them have been employed here for over five years."

It looks like a fairytale out here. Hedges trimmed to look like a maze span out from the house to the river. Walkways break off to unknown places. Flowers spill out in colorful explosions. Giant trees dot the property, beautiful moss hanging from their limbs. And a huge pool breaks off from the side of the ballroom, stretching along the bedrooms on the main level.

But straight ahead, just before the river, is a short fence, surrounding two above ground tombs.

I walk down the stone path that leads to it. It takes me a little while to get there, because the lawn is massive. But I stop just outside the tiny graveyard.

Henry Conrath. Elijah Conrath.

There are no dates. But while my father's tomb is obviously brand new, Elijah's looks like it could be centuries old.

I learned about these once. In places where the water rises too high and there's a risk of bodies and coffins floating to the surface, these tombs or mausoleums are used. Often they're recycled for centuries through the same families. At the back of the tomb is a chamber. Here in the south where it's hot and humid, it only takes about a year or two to decompose a body. When the next family member dies, they re-open the tomb, shove the bones of grandpa into that chamber at the back, and slide in Aunt Jane.

Dozens of people can be endlessly cycled through one tomb.

But I have the feeling that only Elijah and only Henry have occupied these ones.

"How did he die?" I ask Rath. Because I can sense him behind me. Waiting.

"In an accident." Rath says it simply and finally. He'll give me no more details.

I stay there for a few more quiet minutes. Not really feeling anything. Not really thinking anything. Just being.

"Don't let it overwhelm you," Rath says quietly from my side. "All you can do is take it all in one day at a time."

"Right," I say, nodding my head.

The sky bleeds red and gold as the sun sets behind the Mississippi River. The air is hot and humid and oddly comforting.

Home. That's what this place is now. Yet it feels so foreign.

"Would you like me to walk you back to your room?" Rath offers.

I just nod.

Soundlessly, we walk back through the grounds and into the ballroom, out into the grand entryway, and start down the hall. But my eyes catch on an open door and a painting on the wall.

I step into what looks to be a grand library. Filled shelves line the walls, all of them. They open in spaces, leaving room for a sculpture or a painting, and it is one of them that catch my eye.

"Your father was a great man," Rath says. And it's easy to hear the regret and sadness in his voice.

I know I shouldn't touch the painting, but still my fingers reach out to touch his face.

The same strong brows and the same narrow, serious lips. Same dark hair. Our eyes are different, our jaws not quite the same, but still. I look like the offspring of this man.

He was my father and I can't deny that. After all these years, twenty-two of them to be exact, he finally has a face. And it looks like my own.

Without a word, I turn from him and walk out of the library. We turn down the hall, and I open the door to the guest bedroom.

"Thank you," I say to Rath. He nods, and just as he turns to leave, I call out to him. "What room is yours?"

"I don't live in the house," Rath responds with a shake of his head. "The old servants quarters on the property was converted to a workers lodge long ago. I live there with everyone who works at the Estate."

I nod, my eyes starting to glaze over. "So it's just me in the house?"

"That's the way your father preferred it," Rath says.

I nod, feeling something in my stomach sinking. Rath turns to leave again. "Would you mind staying in the house with me? Just for a little while?" I call. He turns back to look at me. "So I'm not alone?"

He looks at me for a long moment. "If you wish, Miss Ryan," he says with a bow.

A bow.

"I will be in the Wayne room," Rath says, indicating the room across and down one from mine. "Should you need anything."

"Thank you, Rath," I say. And I mean it.

He bows one more time, turns, and leaves.

I step in the room and close the door behind me.

The furniture throughout the house has been a mix of extreme classic and modern. An ornate four-poster bed is accompanied by glass-faced nightstands. Across the room is a pink and gold leafed dresser with an ancient jewelry box atop it. The old and the new flow seamlessly.

I open the doors that let out onto the veranda, the pool just feet before it. A soft breeze flutters through, rustling the curtains. I settle into a rocking chair.

Two weeks ago, I got a phone call from an attorney here in Mississippi. The woman on the other line started going off about a Henry Conrath and his passing away. She explained his will, which was helpful. I'd gotten the official, large envelope just the day before and hadn't understood why it had landed in my mailbox.

I was the daughter of a wealthy man from Silent Bend, Mississippi. The daughter of a man I didn't know the name of. And I had just inherited his Estate, his money, everything.

My mother had lived here in Silent Bend for all of three months after getting her associate degree at some community college in Levan—where she'd grown up, an hour east of here. She'd gotten a job here. One night she went to a party where she met a charming man—and one thing led to another.

It was the end of the summer, and she left for college two days later, heading to veterinary school in Colorado. Only three weeks later, she learned she was pregnant and barely remembered the name of the man. But she never said a word to him, and all my life she simply told me that we were strong women—we could do anything on our own.

She *was* strong. Right up until she was killed by a distracted teenage driver playing on a cell phone three years ago.

I was nineteen. Able to take care of myself, live on my own, but still miss her every day.

And then there was the phone call.

Apparently, my mother had told the man who made me that I existed, just a few months before she died, but asked him to not make himself a part of my life so late into my existence.

I wasn't sure if I appreciated that or not.

So, here I am, fulfilling my unknown father's will. I am his only child. So this plantation house is mine. His millions of dollars are mine. His workers and his cars are mine.

I know nothing about him, though. Only that he made me and was rich. No idea how he'd made his money. Nothing of his personality.

It leaves me feeling kind of empty.

Like this house.

I take another deep breath, reminding myself to take this one day at a time.

I close my eyes and imagine myself back in Colorado. Leaving my tiny apartment, with it's old, hand-me-down furniture, slightly *off* smell, heading to work at four in the morning to start the rolls. And the muffins. And the scones. And everything that smelled like comfort.

I'd worked at the bakery for four years. I liked the job. I was good at it. But it could never pay me much, and I could never go anywhere with it.

Well, I'm somewhere now. With more money than I'll ever know what to do with. My entire life had changed.

And there is this constant feeling on my shoulders that something extraordinary is about to happen.

Ewa

FOR A WEEK, I HID on the property. Katina cooked for Rath and I, and the grounds crew and the housekeepers. I made an extra effort to be nice to them, to be polite and sweet, but there was always fear in their eyes whenever they looked at me. I didn't understand that.

I wandered the gardens. Memorized the maze. Made use of the pool.

And I moved into the master suite.

It's grander than me. A massive king-sized canopy bed dominates the room. Ornately carved furniture lines the walls. Beautiful drapes hang in the windows that look out over the river on one side of the room and over the front gardens on the other side.

The space is immense.

But I can feel my father here.

And with every passing day, I feel the hollow hole inside of me growing bigger. I want to know him. I want to know what he was like.

But there is a problem.

Even though this was his house and, as far as I can tell, he'd lived here for a very long time, there is *nothing* personal around. No journals, no letters, no knickknacks. Nothing. The only traces of him I can find are his wardrobe in my closet, that portrait of him in the library, and the fear his staff felt—and has now transferred to me.

Rath had said my father was a great man, so why was everyone else on the property afraid of Henry Conrath?

I want answers.

IT TAKES NINE DAYS FOR me to feel like a self-caged animal. I've been hiding in this mansion to avoid embracing my new Southern life, and I need to be brave.

So on a Monday, at six in the evening, I take a walk down the driveway. It's a long walk. I reach the gates. I climb them. And I keep walking down the road.

This is something I am still getting used to: no mountains here. The land is so flat. Yes, there are small rolling hills dotted around. But I am used to the towering Rocky Mountains.

I swat at a mosquito. They're everywhere. All the time. I quickly learned that repellant is required when stepping one toe outside. I'm regretting not taking one of Henry's vehicles. But it will be a while before I feel comfortable enough to drive them, like they actually belong to me.

On the Conrath plantation, there is the false sense that we are out in the middle of our own world, when really, the minute you turn off the driveway, you pop out onto a road that leads right into town. It is only a quarter mile walk, maybe, before I connect onto Main Street.

Beautiful, old houses line the road, many of them with signs out front marking them as historical sites. I pass a gas station. More houses. Eventually, there are the town's schools. Elementary, middle, and high school all right together. There's a church, a bakery, a few restaurants, a grocery store, two more churches, and finally, city hall, which is attached to the library.

It's a beautiful building. Huge, brick, with a great tower and a bell at the top. A marker with a plaque out front says it was built in 1731, just six years after Silent Bend was established.

My walk into town has been quiet. People are friendly, giving me a tip of their hat as they said hello and offering pleasant smiles, but I didn't really talk to anyone. Which is kind of a relief. I'm still not used to the oftentimes heavy Southern accents.

But I quickly have to get over that when I walk up to the counter in the library.

"Well, you must be new in town," a woman with auburn hair and glasses perched on her nose says as I walk up. The glasses make her look older than I think she really is. "I don't recognize you, and we don't often get tourists wandering into the library."

I offer a little smile and stop at her desk. "Yeah, I just moved in a little over a week ago."

"Well, welcome to Silent Bend," she says with a kind smile. Her accent is strong, but I can at least understand her. "What can I help you with?"

"Uh," I stumble, trying to collect my thoughts. This is my first interaction in my new town—a very small one. I don't want to come off as the wrong type and my request is a strange one. "I was wondering if you might have any information on the Conrath Plantation?"

I was right in hesitating in asking. The woman's face pales and her eyes grow wider.

"The Conrath Plantation?" she questions me. "What interests you in that old place?"

I hesitate in answering. The woman studies me, and I wonder if she's recognizing features in me that my father had. I don't know how well the people in town knew him. It would seem he should be known, since it's a small town, but I get the impression he didn't go out much.

"It's such a beautiful place. I was just curious about it's history," I lie.

She looks at me for a long moment. And I already feel like an outsider in this tiny town. I am an alien here.

"I'll see what I can find for you," she finally says. "But you won't have long. We close in thirty minutes and we don't allow the city record books to be checked out."

"Thank you," I let out in a relieved breath. "I really appreciate it."

She looks over her shoulder back at me one more time as she shuffles off to a back room.

I turn and observe the library.

It's small. Rows of bookshelves are divided in half, one side labeled fiction, the other non-fiction. A row of tables occupy the space between them. I settle myself into the closest one.

A few minutes later, the librarian returns with a large, leather bound book and a copy of what appears to be a newspaper article.

"This is what I could find," she says as she sets them down in front of me. She turns to a marked page in the book.

"Thank you," I say again. "What's your name?"

The woman looks at me, and for the first time, I realize that she seems nervous. Anxious. Suspicious, even. "Bella," she offers.

"I'm Alivia," I say, trying to smooth out the bumps in our meeting, even though I'm not quite sure as to the reason why they're there.

She just gives me a little nod and shuffles away.

My eyes turn down to the page Bella opened for me. At the top of the page, it says clear as day: *Conrath Plantation*. But what is surprising about the page, are the blots of ink, blocking out large portions of the text.

I turn a few pages back and forth. The book seems to be a record and history of all the old houses in Silent Bend, put together by the historical society. But the Conrath page is the only one that seems to have been tampered with.

The two Conrath plantations were bought and purchased by brothers who had recently emigrated from England to the Americas. Bringing with them a large fortune, each brother bought a large parcel of land. They built their separate homes and began to establish cotton plantations.

The plantation established by Henry Conrath is located on the north end of town, and the one established by Elijah Conrath is located on the south.

Each plantation remained in operation until 1875, when Elijah Conrath was killed.

There then are two entire paragraphs inked out.

Little is known about the north plantation after that time. Production was ended and Henry Conrath is rumored to have died soon after his brother.

More blotted out text in that same paragraph. And that brought me to the end of the page.

My father must have been named after his great-something-grandfather. Rath told me the Conrath estate, mine, the north one, was built in 1799. Assuming the south one was built at the same time, Elijah would have been quite old when he was killed.

I wonder who owns the south house now? Did Elijah have his own children he passed it down to? Or has it long since been sold and bought by some stranger?

My fingers reach for the copy of the news article. The title reads "Double Fires."

"I'm sorry, Alivia." I jump hard when the voice cuts through the absolute silence. I turn to see Bella standing behind me. "But we have to close now. You're of course welcome to take the copy with you."

"Okay," I say, swallowing hard, calming the adrenaline in me back. "Thanks again for your help."

She still looks at me with questions and uncertainty as I hand the book over to her. She watches me go as I fold the copy of the article and slide it into my back pocket.

My phone dings when I step outside, and I pull it out to find a text from Rath.

Where are you?

I chuckle. I've never had a father my entire life. I'm twenty-two years old, and my father's former helper man is checking in on me like I'm fifteen.

In town, I reply. *Be back soon.*

It's strange. But kind of nice.

Be back before dark.

Even stranger. And frankly, it kind of annoys me.

I'm a big girl. I can handle myself.

I walk back up Main Street a little ways to the deli I saw earlier and grab myself a sandwich. Everyone is friendly and kind, but in the way that they know they'll forget me in sixty seconds or less. And I realize—everyone in this town thinks I'm a tourist.

On the corner, right next to the Baptist church, I see a sign for a historic walking trail. With little else to do, and not in a hurry to go back to my prison house, I take it and eat my dinner while I walk.

Beautiful houses line the trail. It eventually cuts back toward the river, running right in front of it. Large, early-eighteen hundreds, late-seventeen hundreds houses are everywhere. Nothing compared to the Conrath Estate, but still beautiful.

The trail keeps cutting south, before finally making a loop and heading me back in the direction I came. I wonder how much further south the other Conrath house is.

It's dark by the time I pop back out on Main Street. Lamps glow softly. The street is quiet now, completely empty, which seems weird. I check my phone for the time and find it's just after ten o'clock. Just then, a text comes through.

Rath: *Where are you?*

I'm good and annoyed now. Like a spiteful teenager, I head back down the road, toward the river, the opposite way of home.

As I walk past a house mixed amongst the churches and businesses, a door opens and light floods the sidewalk.

"You got a death wish, girl?" a dark as night woman with a heavy accent shouts. "Do you know what time it is?"

"Excuse me?" I ask, my brows furrowing.

"Get your skinny little rear end inside where it's safe." She looks side to side, her eyes shifty and filled with fear.

And without another word, she slams the door, engulfing me in darkness again.

Weird.

My feet start walking forward again, but my eyes linger on the front door for a good ten steps.

Yeah, it's late. But not that late. Trying to rationalize the woman's warning away, that nothing bad could ever happen in this sleepy little town, I continue my walk down Main Street.

The street runs straight for the river, T-ing right up to it.

And at the end of the road, just before the ground drops down to the river, there is a tree.

Not a single blade of grass grows around it. Pure, uninterrupted dry dirt spreads from its base. A circle of stones, probably twenty feet across, wraps around it.

A heavy, dark feeling creeps into my chest as I look up at the tree. It's enormous, with branches that hang wide and tall, the same as the ones on the Conrath property. But where those trees bare massive leaves, green and brilliant, this one is barren. Not a single sign of greenery to it.

It is completely dead.

But it sits here, the focal point of Main Street, set like a prized sculpture for all to see.

And there's a feeling inside of me. Like bad things had happened here and are still coming. I swear I feel cold fingers working their way up my spine. Bumps flash across my skin.

Because I remember where I've just seen this same tree.

I pull the copy from my back pocket and unfold it. There's the headline, "Double Fires." Beneath that are two pictures. One of a house that looks similar to Henry's. Flames lick out from the windows on one end. And the other picture is of this very same tree. It bears leaves, like it's still alive. But hanging from its massive branches are four bodies.

Three

MY EYES SLIDE FROM THE pictures to the body of the article.

Speculation has run wild following the fires at both Conrath plantations. One witness claims owner Elijah Conrath created an abomination that "had to be destroyed and him with it." Reports show that John Jackson led an attack on the houses, setting fire to them, before dragging Elijah and three of his house members from their home and hanging them from the tree in town.

What followed was a tragedy for the record books.

A hand grabs me around the face, clamping over my mouth just as the scream tries to rip from my throat. The copy flies out of my hand, and as I try to twist away, I feel my phone fall from my pocket. And a fraction of a breath after, a searing pain explodes in my neck.

My body reacts in ways I can't explain. My arms fall limp to my sides. My feet stop trying to run. Worst of all is the way my mind goes numb.

Strong arms hold me upright, holding tight to my upper arm and around my stomach.

This.

This.

What is this?

Logic frantically pounds through my brain, attempting to come up with an explanation that makes sense. But there isn't one.

Someone has bitten me.

Someone is sucking something wet from my neck.

And I can feel it with every passing second—I am going to die.

Beneath a dead tree where four people were hanged. In a bizarre town who fears the night.

I understand the woman's warning now. And Rath's insistence.

I should have listened.

Just as everything starts going fuzzy and my eyelids flutter, I hear something.

A shout, a hiss. A wet thud, and a scream.

The attacker lets go of my neck and I collapse to the ground.

My eyes try to search my surroundings for answers. Anything to bring logic back into reality.

There is a body next to mine. It's a man. Writhing and shifting and twitching in unnatural ways. Gurgled, strangled sounds work their way out of his blood-soaked mouth. There's something protruding from his back.

But most terrifying are his glowing yellow eyes and the black veins covering his face.

"Where'd you come from?"

My eyes shift up just a bit to see a man kneel next to the body. He's young, probably only a few years older than me. In the dark, I can't see any of his features, though. But in his hand is a genuine wooden stake. "Who's your sire?" he demands.

My attacker gives a wet-sounding gasp. He reaches up a hand, like he's about to wrap it around the other man's neck. But his hand shakes and then collapses back onto his chest. His body grows still.

Even though it's dark, I can see the way the color instantly bleeds out of him and his skin turns an ash gray.

"Damnit," the man breathes.

My eyes flutter closed. It takes me a long time to open them again.

When I do, the man is hovering just in my vision.

"Stupid tourists," he says. But his voice sounds hazy, like my ears are full of cotton. "Never know better than to go wandering around after dark in this forsaken town."

"I'm not…" I try to explain, but all the energy in me is gone.

"I'm real sorry about this, but there's not a chance you won't turn," he says. I'm fairly sure I feel his arms slide under me and I'm being lifted. "So you're going to have to stick with me until it's over. Don't worry, I'll make it quick and painless."

"Wh…" my breath leaves my chest. "What?"

"It doesn't usually help to explain," he says. Then there is something hard under my back. It looks like he's putting me in the back of a van of some sort. He leaves and returns a minute later. He lays the other body next to me.

Blackness takes over my vision and my brain fades in and out. But we are moving. Driving. My body screams in pain at every bump we roll over, every jostle that sends me shaking across the hard plastic floor.

Sometime later, maybe ten minutes, maybe an hour—I'm not with it enough to tell, the doors to the van are opened again and I am flooded with unfamiliar scents. Of rotting wood. Stagnant water. Decay and wild earth.

A flashlight blinds my vision and the man is above me.

"Eyes still look normal," he says, flashing the light in and out of my vision. "Pupils still dilating. Why's this taking so long?"

"Please," I say, feeling hot and itchy. "Help me."

"Sorry, darling," he says. I realize then that his accent isn't as overwhelming as many from here. "No one can help you now."

He grabs the dead man next to me, a wooden stake still sticking out of his back. He slings him over his shoulder.

Using everything I have in me, I roll half onto one side and prop myself up on my elbow.

A swamp. That's where we are. I can only faintly make out the standing water in the moonlight, the trees rising up out of it. The moss that holds onto everything.

A slight hissing sound makes my skin crawl.

"Got a nice meal for you tonight, Bernie," the man says. He walks right up to the water's edge and a second later I hear a great splash and a hissing snap. "A nice double-double."

The hissing and snapping grows in intensity, accompanied by a sickening tearing sound.

Flesh.

Snap. Bone.

"Hey now, share, Carl," the man says, and I can almost imagine the sarcastic smile that had to accompany it. "There's plenty for everyone."

Second by second, I feel like my strength is returning and my limbs regain their usefulness. Very slowly, I push myself up onto my forearms, nearly sitting up.

Footsteps crunch over the earth, returning to the van.

"Hey, hey!" he yells, jogging over to me. "Slow it down there. I knew it wouldn't take much longer."

Again, I am blinded by his flashlight. He holds my chin to keep me still as I try to turn my face away.

"What the hell?" he breathes. Over and over, he flashes the light in and out of my eyes.

"Stop," I say, pushing his flashlight away. "My head is already pounding. That is not helping."

"You're getting your strength back," he says, once again flashing the light in my eyes. "You lost way too much blood, though. There's no way you shouldn't be changing. But your eyes, they're still dilating."

"What are you talking about?" I hiss angrily, once again shoving the light away from my face. "And what the hell just happened?"

The man stands straight, his hands on his hips. "Aw shit," he groans. "You're a Born."

"I don't know what that means," I moan. My head is pounding. I push myself up into a sitting position and swing my legs out of the van to dangle to the ground. "But I'd really like to leave now. And find a cop to talk to."

"Not going to do you a bit of good in this town," he says. "Where are you from, and why are you in Silent Bend?"

My fingers rise up to my neck. I fully expect to find shredded skin, the shape of a set of teeth. But the skin is perfectly smooth. Just a slick mess of blood. "I just moved here last week."

"No you didn't," he scoffs and shakes his head. "There are no houses for sale in this town and there are no open rentals."

"Who are you, the real estate police?" I snap back in annoyance. "And I inherited the Conrath Estate for your information, you asshole."

"Excuse me?" he says with complete disbelief. "No, I don't think so. There is no way Henry is dead, and there's not a chance in hell he had any kids."

"Yet here I am!" I yell at him. I work my way onto wobbly legs and take a step toward him. "I've got a will back at the Estate and everything to prove it. I'd invite you over to take a look, but I don't let murderers into my new home!"

"No," he says, shaking his head. "It can't be true." He steps around me and closes the back door of the black utility van. "Get in. We'll go clear this up with Rath right now."

"Great. And when you get confirmation, I'll be contacting the police to have your ass arrested for intending to kill me!"

"If what you say is true, you'll understand why I intended to in about twenty minutes," he hisses as he opens the passenger door for me.

"Why would I get in the car with you?" I shout, throwing my hands up in the air. "We were *just* discussing your intention to kill me!"

"Circumstances have changed," he hisses through clenched teeth. "I promise I won't kill you. So unless you'd like to bunk with the gators for the night, will you please get in the damn car?"

I stare him down, unable to make out any features other than the heat in his eyes. But there isn't murder in them, so, holding his gaze the entire time, I climb in and he closes the door behind me.

There are a million questions frantically racing through my brain as he gets back in the van, starts the engine, and rolls through the swamp. But I can't make sense of a single thought.

I've been attacked. This man killed my attacker. And this man had planned on killing me until something I did changed his mind.

The entire ride back to the Estate is in confused and disbelieving silence.

The second the gates to the Estate come into view, they open. The gravel crunches under our tires and the headlights illuminate the beauty that is the plantation mansion.

Standing out on the porch, hands crossed in front of him, calm and composed, is Rath.

"Is it true?" the man says as we step out of the van and slam the doors shut. "I mean, it can't be, right? Henry's dead and this is his kid?"

"Please, why don't we go inside?" Rath says, calm and composed as ever. But he does give me a narrow, disapproving look.

I doubt the man even heard Rath's request. His eyes are wild and confused and full of adrenaline. He walks into the house first. I meet Rath's eyes and for some reason feel as if I've let him down as I walk past him and into the house.

We end up in the library, only one lamp lit to illuminate the room dimly.

"Rath, how does no one know about this?" the man demands, turning back to face him.

"Because that's exactly the way Henry wanted it," Rath says as he stands behind a wing-backed chair, his hands resting on it.

"Can anyone please tell me what is going on?" I demand, trying to keep the frantic tone out of my voice and totally failing. I am covered in my own blood, after all.

"And she doesn't know a damn thing?" the man says with a breathy laugh and a hand extended out in my direction.

"Lord Conrath wanted to keep it from her for as long as possible, even though he knew it wouldn't take long," Rath says, his tone still even. "And he wished to keep his death a secret, as well."

"Yeah, because the second word got out and anyone saw her, everyone would know the truth."

"*Lord* Conrath? Wh…what? What is happening here?!" I practically scream, and both of their eyes finally turn to me.

"Your father was a damn vampire, that's what," the mystery man yells back at me. "And you're going to be one as well someday."

It takes about eleven seconds for the word to register in my brain and to process what it means.

It takes about four more seconds for the laugh to break from my chest. It builds and builds until I must look completely hysterical.

"Miss Ryan," Rath says, loud enough to be heard over my meltdown. "Mr. Ward is telling the truth."

"Come on, Rath," I continue laughing. "You don't seem the type to pull pranks, but you got me. It was awful and I think you two might be completely insane, but you got me good."

"This isn't a joke," the man with at least a last name now says. There's actual offense in his voice. And I now finally register him. I was right, he's probably only a few years older than me. Wild, slightly too long brown hair on his head. Dark eyes under dark, heavy brows. Thin, serious lips. Intense five o'clock shadow. "Do you not remember how that blood got all over you? That thing was trying to suck you dry before I staked it. Remember how I said I was going to kill you, too? That's because that bite should have turned you."

My laughter dies away as my hand once again rises to my neck. I finally look down at myself. My clothes are drenched in my blood. Dirt is sticking to me all over. I'm a wreck. I remember the numbness that took me over within seconds of the pain.

"We're telling the truth," Rath says. His voice is kind and quiet. "Your father was a vampire and immortal Born. He spent a night with a human woman, and you were conceived."

Vampires. Being Born. Stakes.

I want to call bullshit. But what just happened to me had happened.

And these two guys are staring at me without even a hint of uncertainty in their eyes.

"Why didn't you say anything when I got here?" I accuse Rath. My eyes burn as I look at him.

"Because that was your father's wish." He turns from me to a desk against one wall. He takes a key from his pocket and opens a drawer. From it, he pulls a letter. The back of it is sealed with a wax stamp. "He asked me to give this to you when the time was right."

My hands shake as I take it. The envelope that bears my name— Alivia Ryan—on the front is immediately smeared with my blood and dirt. There's more weight to it than just a few pieces of paper. There's something hard inside.

"Rath, you know what this means, right?" Mr. Ward says quietly. "There's no way the House won't hear about the attack tonight. They're going to find out and quickly. They'll want to take her in."

"I know." I look up and see Rath staring straight at me. "We don't have much time."

"Look, I can help," Mr. Ward says, and his voice sounds desperate. "Let me talk to her. Because if the House gets to her first, they'll manipulate her and she'll have no real choice of her own."

"You're right," Rath says. He takes a few steps across the room and places his hands on my shoulders. "But first, you need to clean up and get some rest. You look like shit, my dear."

And his unexpected word drags my eyes up to his.

Rath is cold and quiet and distant. But I see it in his eyes. He doesn't really know me at all, but he cares about me. And I feel the emotion being reciprocated in me.

"Ian, you're welcome to stay in any of the rooms on the main level until morning," Rath says over his shoulder as he leads me from the room and toward the stairs.

"Are you serious?" Ian Ward yells from behind us. "You're going to cut off the momentum, just like that?"

"Just like that," Rath says as we step onto the second floor.

I don't know what to expect from the rest of the night, probably a long study of the ceiling in my room, but I'm curious as hell and scared to death to see what morning brings.

Four

"RISE AND SHINE, PRINCESS."

My eyes fly open to a face just inches from mine. My instincts wake before my brain and my fist flies to clip the edge of a jaw. A crushing hand wraps around my fist, though, and holds it stationary.

"Nice reflexes," Ian Ward says as he lets go of my hand and takes half a step away from my bed. "Maybe you have half a chance of surviving the week."

"What are you doing in my room?" I hiss, swinging my legs out of the bed and taking an aggressive step toward him. It's when his eyes drop down that I remember that I only pulled on one of Henry's t-shirts before collapsing into bed after a shower last night.

Too late for modesty. Ian's seen me in all my glory.

"Rath was going to let you sleep all day, but we've got stuff to talk about. Training to start," Ian says as his eyes linger on my exposed legs for just a moment longer. When his eyes come back to mine, I notice how beautiful they are for the first time. They're hazel, but bright and dark at the same time. And bear no shame in staring.

"Training," I repeat. "What are you, some kind of sensei?"

"I won't object to it if you want to call me that," he says with a lopsided little smile.

"In your dreams," I say with a raised eyebrow. He's staring at me and I'm staring at him, thinking how unbelievable he is considering he wanted to kill me last night. I take a step around him and head for the massive closet. The housekeeper hung my clothes up next to Henry's. She had asked if I wanted them put away, and I told her no. I didn't have a reason for leaving them, but I didn't want them to disappear, too, just like Henry did.

I pull on a pair of sweat shorts, feeling Ian's eyes on me the entire time.

"How old are you?" Ian asks as I turn back to face him and lean in the doorway.

"I turned twenty-two on New Year's Day."

"So everyone parties the same day you do," Ian says, crossing his arms over his chest with a small smile again.

I shrug. "And how old are you, master vampire slayer?"

"Twenty-four," he answers.

Someone knocks on the already open door, and we both turn to see the cook. "Breakfast is ready, if you're hungry." She doesn't meet either of our eyes when she says it.

"Great, I'm starved and the day's already half gone." Ian walks out the door without a second glance.

The stairs creak just slightly as we both descend them. For the past ten days I've been here, I've insisted on eating my meals in the informal dining room adjacent to the kitchen. But helpers walk in and out of the formal dining room.

"Pretty swanky place you inherited," Ian says as we both slip in behind them. Rath is already seated at the table, a cup of coffee and a newspaper before him.

"What, you don't live in a mansion, too?" I ask Ian sarcastically as I slide into a chair, one leg bent up. My manners are shocking here in the South.

Ian gives an awkward chuckle and his eyes drop away as he sits, as well. "Not exactly."

And for some reason I feel embarrassed for my response. There's something about Ian that brings out a sharp edge I didn't know I had to me.

"I hope you got some rest," Rath says as he folds his paper and sets it on the table. He looks up at me as he takes a sip of his coffee.

"Eventually, yeah," I say as I reach for a scoop of fresh fruit and a biscuit. "Pretty sure I had some crazy dreams last night, though." All of last night felt completely insane.

"Understandable," Rath says with a little nod of his head.

"Enough with the formalities," Ian breaks in. His table manners aren't any better than mine. He's got one leg swung over the arm of the ornate dining chair, his dirty boot hanging in the air for all to see. "Can we get down to business?"

"For being from the South, your manners are atrocious," Rath tells him through clenched teeth. "Most would find it inappropriate to discuss the intricacies of the vampire world over breakfast."

"Breakfast seems as good a time as any to talk insanity," I say before I take a huge bite out of the biscuit. I then see the gravy that was supposed to go over the top of it.

I have so much to learn about my new world—and not just about vampires.

"See, she gets it," Ian says. And he freaking winks at me.

"Very well," Rath says, wiping his already spotlessly clean hands on a napkin. "I suppose we'll start from the very beginning."

I pop a few grapes in my mouth and angle myself toward him.

"Some several thousand years ago, a man named Cyrus was a bit of a scientist, you could say. Not many details have survived the millennia, but somehow he found a way to make himself the ultimate predator—and immortal. The very first vampire. He was stronger, faster, better than everyone around him. At first he thought himself the pinnacle of human perfection. But he also craved blood, from his own past kind. Ignoring the horror of the last fact, he desired that his wife become like him."

I take a drink of my orange juice, but it doesn't taste right. I swear I taste a hint of copper and rust. I look down in my cup to make sure it hadn't changed to blood.

"His wife, however, was afraid of what her husband had become. While he was strong, healthy, and incredible, a more enhanced version of his previous self, but he was also brutal, a more enhanced version of his previous self. He'd attacked people, killed them as he drained them of blood." Rath's eyes have drawn inward, as if seeing the story he's painting. "She loved him, despite his flaws. But she wasn't sure she wanted to be like him."

Rath takes another draw of his coffee. "In the end, Cyrus changed her anyway through the same process. What he did not know, though, was that she was with child."

Something cold snakes its way up my spine. Something dreadful and so very wrong.

"Sevan conceived as a human and gave birth as a vampire."

"What was the baby?" I ask. I didn't realize until now that I'm sitting forward, nearly on the edge of my seat. "The baby was born a vampire?"

Rath shakes his head. "The child was born seemingly human. Ate, lived, looked exactly as every other human out there. Two unique, genesis vampire parents with a human baby. Everything seemed right and natural. Until the child died just after his eighteenth birthday."

My brows furrow and the room is so silent, I hear it when Ian scratches at his jawline.

"They buried their son. Mourned over him. But then, just four days later, he rose from the grave."

I swear under my breath. Ian looks over at me, but he doesn't have that mischievous smile on his lips like what I'm learning is so common for him. He's as dead serious as that son should have been.

"The son resurrected as a vampire. Exactly the same as his parents."

"That's why you called me a Born, isn't it?" I ask as I look back at Ian.

He nods. "Only a Born could recover from a bite like you did. Anyone else would have turned."

"The son resurrected as himself," Rath continues the story. "And after a few years, they all realized he was not aging. He, too, was immortal. Realizing what he was and what he had defied, he became obsessed with creating others like himself. He took many women for himself. Horrifically, some of them conceived. Not all, but enough. Children were born. And once each of them reached their prime age, he killed them all."

"That's awful," I say in shock. This man, father and murderer in the same breath. The thought is terrifying.

Both Rath and Ian are looking at me with a weight I don't quite understand.

"The Born were not the only new creature to walk the earth, though," Rath continues. "Those that Cyrus had bitten and nearly killed turned into something new. Different than Cyrus and his family. They still aged. They craved blood more than the Born. Without it, they withered and died. They were the Bitten. They had never died, but they would. Their lifespans were the same as if they'd lived as a normal human."

We've been in this room for quite some time now, and I just now realize that not a single attendant has re-entered the room since Rath began his story.

I'm starting to understand now why they look at me with fear in their eyes.

"The son had created seven sons of his own and eight daughters. But still he wanted more. He wished for an army to dominate those around him. He was cruel and reckless. Seeing what his son had become and the threat he posed to his reign, Cyrus killed him."

"But I thought the Born were immortal?" I ask leaning forward, my forearms on the table. "How did he kill his son?"

"A few of the stories you hear about vampires are true," Ian says, resting his forearm over the edge of the arm of the chair.

"A stake through the heart," I say, recalling what Ian had done last night.

Rath nods. "Cyrus' son was dead, but the damage was done. There were seven more Born vampires with the ability to create more offspring."

"What about the female Born?" I ask.

Rath shakes his head. "Once resurrected, a female Born can not reproduce."

"So a Born can only be created with a human mother and a vampire father?" I ask to clarify.

"You got it," Ian confirms.

"Cyrus is still alive," Rath says, moving things along. "And he rules as King over all vampires."

"The vampires have a king?" I repeat, raising one eyebrow. This all just keeps getting layered deeper and deeper in the crazy.

"King Cyrus is ancient and thorough. To this day, he and his attendants keep tabs on all the royal male lines."

"Why?" I ask.

"That is a story for another day," Rath says. And suddenly he seems exhausted. It's a heavy tale to tell and one I think has been weighing him down for a long time.

Is Rath a Born vampire?

Or an all too well informed human?

"Wow," I say, feeling overwhelmed and a bit like everything I've just learned is going to fuzz my brain out. "Okay. There's complicated history in the vampire world. And I know there's some deep history to this house. But, Rath, I have to ask. How did my father really die?"

"I think we'd all like to know the answer to that question." Ian finally sits upright, leaning forward, elbows on the table, fingers tightly locked together.

Rath's eyes grow distant and dark. There's anger there. Hate. Regret.

"It was just as the sun was coming up," he begins. "Your father was preparing to go to sleep. I was just waking, still in the workers house." He stops talking for a while. Takes a few slow breaths. "Someone broke in. Got past the security systems. They staked your father and drug his body out into the sun as he lay dying. I arrived at the scene as he took his last breath."

Rath holds a fork in his hands, and he's now bent it completely in half.

"I should have chased the attacker down, ended them. But I was…not in my right mind, after I found Henry. They got away."

"Who was it?" Ian asks. His voice is low and serious. "Someone from the House?"

Rath shakes his head. "I did not recognize the attacker. The fact that they were able to take Henry down so easily says a great deal, though."

He suddenly slaps the destroyed fork on the table, and I jump violently.

The message is clear. We are done talking about my father's death.

"Okay," I say, because it is obviously time to move onto something new. "Um…what about the turning into a bat thing?"

"Rumor," Ian tells me with a slight roll of his eyes. He too seems to understand that the previous conversation is finished. "A seriously stupid one."

"Okay," I say with a nod of my head. "You said the stake through the heart is true. The beheading thing has to be, as well."

Ian nods in confirmation.

"What about the sun?" I ask. "Do they really burn up in the sun?" I try not to think about how the attacker dragged my father out into the sunlight and what must have happened to him.

"Not like you'd think," Rath says with a bit of a sigh. "The vampires have an extreme aversion to the sun because when they turn, their eyes change. We do not understand the science behind what the King put in his concoction that created the species, but it is a mix of predator DNA. They take good and bad traits from many different hunters. Vampires do love the night particularly because their eyes stay almost completely dilated. You could compare them much to a bat, I suppose. They can see almost perfectly at night. But because of the dilation, their eyes can not stand much sun."

"They can go out during the day," Ian says. "But not without some serious shades and a killer headache."

"But no burning skin?" I ask.

"No burning, flaming bodies," he says, that mischievous smile returning as he shakes his head. "They're fast, strong like a bear, tough as a rhino, and quiet as cats. They really are the evolution of the perfect predator."

I nod, feeling like I'm starting to get a small grasp on this whole thing. "Okay, so the Born are immortal, the Bitten age as normal. Both can be killed with a stake to the heart or a quick beheading. There's a King who sounds pretty badass. My father was a Born vampire, my mother was a human, which means when I die…" My words slow as all the puzzle pieces start falling into their right order. "I'm not really going to die…"

I say this last part slowly because it's only now that I'm starting to realize the impact of what I just said.

"I'm going to be a vampire someday," I breathe.

"I'm afraid so," Rath says quietly.

But it's Ian who surprises me when I look up. His eyes are intense and dark and conflicted.

There's so much to him that I don't understand.

"Alright," I say with a deep breath. "Anything I'm missing?"

This brings the smile back to Ian's face. "Oh, baby doll, we've barely scratched the surface."

Five

"THE BAGS ARE PACKED." BETH, one of the housekeepers, interrupts the all too quiet dining room. I turn to see her not quite looking at any of us, holding a packed suitcase in her hands.

"Thank you," Rath says. She gives an uncomfortable smile, leaves the bag on the floor, and leaves.

I turn questioning eyes on Rath, who stares at me for a bit longer than he should to be innocent.

"Mr. Ward and I talked last night while you slept and came to a decision," Rath starts. He places his elbows on the table and laces his fingers together. "As he mentioned last night, there is no way the House won't hear about your attack. They will come for you and while I don't believe it will be to the extreme that Ian does, they will sway you with you being so uninformed, and I know your father wouldn't have wanted that."

"What do you mean by house?" I ask, every survival instinct in me perking up. I don't like where this is heading.

"Ian will educate you as you start training," Rath says. He snaps his fingers and attendants flood into the room to begin clearing breakfast. "But for now, we both feel it best that you stay away from the Conrath Estate until you are ready. You will be going to stay with Ian."

My head whips to look at him, and I'm sure a sour expression dominates my face. "You're kidding, right? We've already established how he tried to kill me, and you want to send me off to live with him?"

"Mr. Ward will bring you no harm," Rath says as he stands. Ian and I do at the same time, as well. "He didn't know the circumstances at the time, and he did what he thought best. Trust me, no one will be more skilled in keeping you safe until you are ready to make your own decisions."

"Decisions about what?" I demand. I back toward the door. I don't know what I'm going to do: run, hide, head back to Colorado—but I don't like feeling like I do.

"The decision about whether you want to join the House or not," Ian says impatiently. He walks around the table and grabs the bag from the floor. "Can you just take my promise that I won't hurt you and get going? We really don't have a whole lot of time. It's already uncomfortably far into the afternoon."

I look at the clock hanging on the far wall and realize that despite having just eaten "breakfast," it is four in the afternoon. Rath really was going to let me sleep all day.

My eyes flick between Ian and Rath and back again.

I don't know what to do.

I barely know these men. I don't know whom to trust.

But there's an echo in the back of my head saying that this is what my father would have wanted. And even though I didn't know him at all, I feel like I would have wanted to.

"You're not really giving me a choice, are you?" I ask, feeling the fight seep out of me.

"Not when you don't understand the big picture yet." Ian's eyes are begging me to trust him. And there's something there in the purse of his lips, in the tenseness of his shoulders, in the readiness of his stance that makes me think I can.

"Let me go get dressed," I say resentfully.

Stranger danger is screaming at me the whole time I'm getting ready. But it's a tiny thing pushed into the corner by an attack last night and a very big story told over breakfast. So I slide into shorts and a t-shirt, and knot my hair on top of my head. Lastly, I slide the unopened letter from my father into my back pocket.

"We should get going," Ian says as I come down the stairs. He's already waiting by the front door, keys in hand, my bag in the other.

I nod and turn to Rath.

"I'm putting a lot of trust in you," I say. My eyes are begging for him to say I can stay, to take everything from the past twenty-four hours back. Somehow I feel like he should have that power. Even though that's stupid.

"I know," he says. And to my surprise, he wraps his arms around me in a brief hug. "This is for the best."

When I let go of him, I don't meet his eyes. I turn for the door, open it, and walk straight out.

Ian's van is one of those utility kinds with no windows in the back. It's black and covered in mud and grime. I'd wager it's got traces of blood on it somewhere—likely some of my own.

I open the passenger door and climb in.

Ian throws my bag into the back where, only last night, I had lain bloody and muddy and climbs into the driver's seat. Without a word, he turns around and starts down the drive.

When we pop out onto the main road, we take a left instead of a right into town. Ian slips out his phone and dials someone.

"Hey, Phil, it's Ian," he says as he takes a right and we're heading south. "Yeah, I'm not feeling so hot today so I'm going to need someone to cover my shift tonight. Yeah, I know this is the second time this month, but what can I say? You get around a lot of sickness, you tend to get sick. Yeah. Gotcha. 'K, thanks."

He hangs up and slides the phone back into his pocket.

"You have a job outside of vampire hunting?" I ask skeptically.

"Of course I have a job," he says, giving me an offended look. "You think it pays the bills to keep vamps off the streets of Silent Bend? I gotta' eat, just like all the other ignorant people."

"Sorry," I say, holding my hands up in surrender. "It's just... mundane, hearing that someone like you has a job. What do you do?"

"I'm an EMT," he says as he looks out the front window. The trees get thicker and heavier around the road. I have the feeling we're not too far from the swamps I so pleasantly got to visit last night.

"Also surprising," I say with a nod. "Though I have to say, knowing you're tangled up with vampires kind of makes me wonder if you're some kind of supplier of blood to them."

Ian cuts me an ice-cold look. "I'd never."

"Sorry," I immediately apologize. It's going to take me some time to learn my boundaries with Ian Ward.

He doesn't say anything else as we continue our drive.

I was right. This seems like swampland, and I'm sure that at any minute, we'll be sloshing through water and have alligators jump out at us from the stagnant swamps.

But we stay on the road and turn off onto an even scarier-looking one.

The trees with endless amounts of moss hanging from them threaten to swallow us for a minute, almost totally blocking out the sun. But suddenly, we break out into a clearing. No swamp, just well-trimmed grass and a little yellow house with flower gardens out front.

It's picturesque.

"This is your house?" I ask in shock.

"It's my grandmother's house," Ian says as he continues on the little dirt road stretching to the side of it. We continue on for a while longer, back into more trees, and stop in front of what looks like a tiny cabin or a shed. It's rustic, and looks like it's been put together in stages, but it has a certain manly charm to it. "This is my house."

Ian turns off the engine and climbs out. He grabs my bag from the back as I climb out and marvel at the complex beauty around me.

Massive trees dot the landscape here and there, blocking out the sun with their giant leaves. Spanish moss hangs long and thick from the branches. Undergrowth hides unknown trails. The sun trickles through to dot the tin roof of Ian's house. I look back at the yellow house. It's so charming and bathed in sunlight. Like something out of a fairytale.

The two houses are polar opposites.

"Alivia?" Ian calls from his front porch. "You coming?"

"Yeah," I say quietly. I turn and follow him inside.

The walls are all wood and everything looks used or salvaged. I'd honestly be kind of shocked if Ian didn't build this place with his own hands. A small living room with a worn-out couch and a rocking chair occupy the right side of the space. To the left is a small simple kitchen. Straight ahead I can see into a bedroom and there's a bathroom.

This is almost exactly the same size as my apartment in Colorado, and I find it oddly comforting.

"It's not much to look at, but it's my own space," Ian says as he walks back from the bedroom where he's just set my bag on the bed. "Started building it when I was only fifteen. Finished it a few years back."

I was right.

"It's a far cry from Conrath Estate, but the House will never come looking for you here."

"Right," I say as I wander to the bedroom. There's a queen-sized bed with a worn-out blue comforter on it. A dresser is pushed up next to the closet and that's all that occupies the space. The bathroom isn't any bigger than necessary to cram in a shower, toilet, and sink.

"Don't worry," Ian says as he stuffs his hands in his pockets and observes me. "I'll take the couch."

My polite instinct is to say that he doesn't have to. It's his house and his bed, not mine. But then again, this was his idea, and Rath's, and if not for that idea, I'd be sleeping in my suite and not putting anyone out.

"Okay," I say simply.

I jump pretty violently when there's a knock on the closed front door before it opens.

I turn to find a pretty, young blonde girl staring at me with startled eyes. "Oh," she says. "I'm sorry, I uh…didn't realize Ian had company." The shocked and confused tone to her voice tells me how rare of an occasion this truly is.

"Elle, this is Alivia Ryan," Ian says, waving a hand in my direction. "Alivia, this is my little sister, Elle Ward."

"Oh," I say, surprised once again by this vamp hunter. "I…uh, it's nice to meet you."

"I love your name," Elle says shyly with a smile that looks so much like Ian's. She tucks a lock of hair behind her ear. "Ian, Lula told me to tell you it's time for dinner."

"'K," he says. "We'll be right in."

Elle looks at me one more time and offers a fluttering little smile before she heads outside again.

"I should have figured you were a big brother," I say with a small smile when I meet his eyes. "You do have that whole protective quality going on."

Ian fights off a smile and opens the door wider for me. "Shut up," he laughs. "Come on. Don't make my grandmother wait for us."

The house is as warm and inviting inside as it looks from the outside. Crisp white walls, a light, sky blue ceiling. Old, well worn, but taken care of furniture. It smells like a grandma, but in all the right ways. It makes me wish I'd had a grandmother. My own died when I was only six years old.

We round the corner of the living room into the dining room and kitchen. Elle is helping a woman set things on the table.

"Lula, I hope you don't mind that I have a guest tonight," Ian says as he places his hands on the back of a chair. I stand there uncomfortably.

The woman turns, and I see her face for the first time.

It's impossible not to notice the wrinkles first. Folds and canyons and ravines cover her entire body. Dark eyes are hooded and shadowed by her features. Her earlobes are long and dangly. And unlike the kind, motherly woman I was expecting from the house, this woman's eyes are fierce and dark.

"You got a girlfriend?" she asks, somehow managing to raise an eyebrow as she shuffles across the kitchen to the table with a casserole dish in her weathered hands. Her Southern drawl is strong, and I can barely understand her.

"Uh," Ian says uncomfortably, scratching the back of his neck. "No. This is Alivia Ryan. She just got into town."

The woman looks at me, staring me down like she can see into my soul.

"It's nice to meet you," I say without squirming.

Finally, she gives a grunt and a nod before turning back to retrieve something from the kitchen.

"Don't worry about her," Ian whispers in my ear. His closeness makes something in my stomach do a backflip. "She's pretty crazy and won't even remember you were here in the morning."

"She really won't," Elle says quietly as she finishes setting the table.

"Oh," is all I can say in this super awkward situation.

After saying grace, everyone digs into their dinner.

"School starts on Monday, right Elle?" Ian asks around a mouthful of some kind of food that's so Southern I don't have a name for it. Since we ate only an hour ago, I'm having a hard time fitting anything else in my stomach.

She nods. "Sophomore year," she says with a cringe. "Do you think you could drive me into town to get the rest of my stuff tomorrow?"

"I'll take 'ya, child," Lula says. "Been takin' care of 'ya fo' the last how many years? I'll keep on keepin' on."

"Yes, Lula," Elle says, looking down at her plate with a knowing little smile.

I glance over at Ian. His eyes flit over to mine. "She can't drive anymore, and hasn't been able to for quite a few years. Thankfully, her hearing isn't what it used to be either."

I look back at her, and she's staring at her food, munching slowly and deliberately.

We finish our meal and Lula shuffles off to bed, even though it's barely seven o'clock. Elle clears the table as Ian and I do the dishes.

"How old is your grandmother?" I ask when we're nearly finished and Elle has said goodnight to go read a book.

"She's eighty-seven," Ian says as he dries the last plate and puts it away. I drain the dishwater and dry my hands. Together we walk out to the back porch and sit on the top stair.

"She's Elle's caretaker, isn't she?" I ask quietly as the sun starts to slip toward the trees.

Ian nods. His eyes drop to the steps we sit on. His forearms rest on his knees, his fingers tightly knitted together.

"What happened to your parents, Ian?"

He chews the inside of his lip for a second, and I can feel the gears turning in his head. He picks at a hangnail before finally answering me.

"We lived in this little, crappy house closer to town when I was a kid. It always smelled like swamp, even though we were miles from it. One night when I was ten, I was lying awake, listening to my parents fight for the thousandth time. They fought all the time. Elle was sleeping on the bottom bunk, even though she probably should have been in a crib—she was only two, snoring like a wolf." He chuckles, his eyes rising to the horizon, and shakes his head.

"There was a loud shatter, like the door being busted down. My mom screamed and dad yelled. There were gunshots." He swallows and his eyes fall back down again. "I was scared, scared to death. But I climbed out of bed and cracked open the door. It looked right out into the living room. What I saw…there wasn't any logical explanation for it to a ten year old."

I know what's coming and imagining the scene? It's horrific. I fight the urge to reach out and rub a hand over Ian's back.

"There was this man there," he says, his voice hardening, but showing the slightest emotion. "Eyes glowing red, face covered in these horrible black veins. His face was covered in blood. Dad was already dead, drained dry. The vampire was holding Mom. She was stone white."

A shiver runs up my back. As horrible as my own mother's death had been, at least I hadn't witnessed her murder. In such a brutal and unnatural way.

"The vamp looked up at me, and I thought for sure I was dead. Elle, too. I should have screamed, but I could only stare at my dead mom." His voice cracks just slightly, but overpowering it is anger. "The thing just stared at me…for a long time. Finally, sense came back to my brain. I slammed the door shut, locked it. I grabbed Elle from her bed. She started crying. I crawled out the window with her and started running." Ian takes a deep breath, his eyes rising back up. "I ran here. To my grandmother's house. I told her what I'd seen. The crazy thing was that she believed me."

Finally, hesitantly, I reach out and place a hand on his back. His body is warm through his t-shirt. I rub my hand back and forth lightly just twice.

Ian had been just a kid. He was so young and so innocent. And in an instant, he'd become an orphan. But instead of crying, instead of breaking down like pretty much anyone else would have, he grabbed his baby sister and saved both of their lives.

Ian looks back at me, his eyes serious and heavy. "You hear that ignorance is bliss all the time. I had no idea as a kid how bad Silent Bend's vampire problem was. And is. And the thing is, half the town is fully aware of it."

"Whatever this House is that you keep saying is going to come after me, they're all vampires, aren't they?" I ask, taking my hand back.

Ian nods and then stands. He reaches out a hand and pulls me to my feet. "Yeah. And I'll tell you about them, but first we have to lock the house down."

When we walk back inside, Ian makes his way to Elle's bedroom. "You need to go anywhere else tonight?" he asks.

She looks up from her book, lying on her bed, and shakes her head.

"'K," Ian says. "I'm going to lock up now. We're going to bed."

"Alright," she says, glancing over at me. But it isn't suggestive, considering what Ian just said. This girl knows her brother. It comforts me that she knows Ian isn't like that. "Goodnight."

"Night," he says as he pulls her door closed.

I wait in the living room as Ian tells his grandmother goodnight. And as I wait, I then realize how there are bars on all the windows in the house.

Ian reemerges and heads straight for the front door. He sets a series of locks that are intense. He does the same for the side door that goes out the laundry room. "Come on," he says with the tip of his head for the back door. We walk out and he pulls out keys and locks no less than four locks. Finally, he pulls out his phone and taps something. I hear three beeps from inside. A green light flashes on one of the locks.

"That's one intense security system," I say as he slips his phone back into his pocket. "I'm guessing that doesn't alert the authorities if it's tripped."

Ian shakes his head. "You'd guess right."

Poor Elle. Considering all of this, it's hard to imagine she's capable of having much of a social life. Or any chance at any form of a normal life at all.

We walk across the lawn and back in to the cabin. I flip a light on and turn to watch Ian lock up six locks, sliding a solid iron bar over the door.

"Will all that stuff really keep out a vampire if they're determined to get in?" I ask.

Ian turns to look at me. "Not if they really want to get in. But it'll slow them down. Take a look."

Ian walks over to his couch and pulls the cushions off of it. Beneath them is a long box, the entire length of the couch. He pulls off the lid.

Inside is a huge stack of wooden stakes. Some of them stained with blood.

"You take being a vigilante seriously," I say, raising an eyebrow.

He actually laughs. He gets small crinkle lines around his eyes and mouth when he does. It's kind of ridiculously charming. "You have no idea, baby doll."

He's called me that twice now...

He crosses to the kitchen and opens the oven. But instead of delicious baked goods, this one reveals a stash of guns and knives. Ian looks back at me and gives a smug look. He goes on to reveal a mirror in the bathroom that opens to show off more guns. From beneath his bed he pulls out a crossbow and three shotguns.

"Okay, I realize now why Rath sent me off to stay here," I say. There's genuine concern in my voice. I'm suddenly very intimidated.

"I'm not letting another vamp touch my family again," Ian says seriously as he slides the shotguns back under the bed. "It's been pretty safe in this town the last two years or so, but your attack? Henry's? They were both out of place."

"How so?" I ask, settling onto the bed. It's well worn out. I can feel the springs.

"Look, Liv," he says, rubbing his eyes with a thumb and a finger. "There's a lot to educate you on and not a whole ton of time to do it. But I'm exhausted and have been up for the last two nights straight. I'll make more sense in the morning."

I glance outside. There's still plenty of light on the horizon, I'd guess it's not even nine o'clock. But he does look exhausted.

"Okay," I say. "We can talk in the morning."

He rubs his eyes again and doesn't even look at me before peeling off the wall and disappearing into the bathroom. I lie back on the bed and stare at the wooden ceiling, listening to him preparing for bed. A few minutes later, he walks out and back into the bedroom.

"I may be a Southern gentleman and offered my bed, but you've got to share the pillows," he says with an attempt of a smile. But it's tired.

I grab one and throw it at him.

He catches it, reflexes quick and agile. He offers an appreciative smile and heads for the couch in the living room. Not five minutes later, I hear a faint snore drifting in through the door.

This all seems so overkill. Having to leave the home I just learned I had. Hiding in a cabin in the woods with a guy who has an obsession with weapons and bloodsuckers.

But my hand reaches up to where I was bitten. I'd wandered out of the house *once* and was almost immediately attacked.

There's so much more to Silent Bend than meets the eye.

I roll onto my side and feel something hard press into my rear end. Remembering the letter in my back pocket, I pull it out.

My name is written in elegant script, curving and bending in ways that isn't often seen in this century.

Thinking back to what that book said about Henry Conrath building the plantation house in 1799, I know now that it wasn't his great-something-grandfather. It was my father.

I slide my finger under the wax seal and break the raven crest. I pull two sheets of paper from inside it, and an ornate, old fashioned key with a raven set in the middle of the handle falls out into my hand.

Setting the key on my chest, my eyes turn to the letter.

My dear Alivia,

I've thought about the contents of this letter for over a month now. In my grand perspective of time, it's really nothing more than the blink of an eye, but still, it's been on my mind every waking second.

Your mother tracked me down and told me of your existence. I must admit that I couldn't really believe her at first. You see, it isn't an easy thing for someone like me to create offspring. And it's been a long time since I last saw Marlene Ryan. But she sent me your picture and I knew. I see it with my own eyes. I am your father.

And that knowledge fills me with both great elation and solemn regret. I've lived a life of isolation for a very long time because losing my only family member has destroyed me in ways I never could have imagined. So knowing that for the past nineteen years I have in fact had family makes me so happy. I wish I had known sooner. I wish we could have had time together. I wish I could have been there for you.

I don't realize that I'm crying, just a few paragraphs in, until a strangled breath catches in my throat and a tear rolls down my cheek and drips back into my ear. All my insides are shaking, quivering. My chest feels tight and constricted.

I have many wishes for what might have been.

But I am also sorry.

Knowing that I am your father, I know the fate that I have put upon your shoulders. Eventually, you will know the truth about what I am. It may take years, hopefully many, many of them. But what I have is yours, and someday, I suppose, you will learn everything.

I am sorry I have thrust you into this immortal life. My own has been a long one, and the vast majority of it has been unhappy. It's been full of politics and manipulation and distrust. I never want that for you.

So I ask you this: stay away from the House. Stay away from the King. Stay away from our kind.

I know this is asking for a life of isolation, but I only found peace when I removed myself from everything I've just listed out for you. They can bring you nothing but pain.

Should you ever come to Silent Bend and I am no longer alive, I've asked Rath to give you this letter. I had hoped that we could meet some day, face to face. But I am a coward. If you're reading this, it means I never found the courage to seek you out myself and do it the right way. There are not enough sorrys that I can put on these pages for that.

But if you come, trust Rath. He will never lead you astray. His loyalty is unprecedented, and he will take care of you.

I wish I could have gotten the same opportunity.

I know we've never met, but I do love you, Alivia.

Until we meet, all my love,

Henry.

I will do my best, Henry. I promise.

Six

"RISE AND SHINE, PRINCESS."

I breathe the words right into Ian's ear. When he lashes out with a fist, I hold up the frying pan, blocking his blow. But he springs off the couch faster than I expect, diving for my legs. I go down on top of him with a yelp. Determined not to be bested, I twist, wrapping my legs around his neck and attempting to squeeze.

But Ian is a rolling, writhing snake and he springs to his feet. I dangle with my legs still wrapped around his neck, the two of us back to back, me hanging upside down.

For half a second, a smile crosses my lips.

But with a great yell, Ian flips me over his shoulder. I manage to twist slightly as he does and land on my back. Hard.

Ian pins me to the ground, forearm across my throat, clutching a stake in his hand. He pants, eyes wild and wide. They go even wider when he realizes it's me.

"What do you think you're doing?" he asks as confusion takes over his expression. But his voice is loaded with annoyance.

"Trying to prove I'm not a useless little flower," I say with a snide smile. Ian is shirtless, his bare skin pressed up against my stomach since my shirt has ridden up during our wrestling match. "I may not know how to defend myself yet, but I'm not all that delicate, either."

Ian stares at me, his eyes going back and forth between mine. And slowly, a smile chips its way onto his lips. He lets out a little chuckle. "Yeah, you're Henry's daughter, all right. He was a defiant little prick, too."

"I'll take that as a compliment," I say as Ian stands and pulls me to my feet.

"What time is it?" Ian asks.

"Clock in your room says nine-thirty," I say as I move to the kitchen. I'm starving, and that was one of the main reasons I woke Ian. "I figured twelve and a half hours of sleep should be enough."

"Damn," Ian says as he shuffles off to the bathroom. "Can't remember the last time I slept that long." He only half shuts the door before he starts taking a leak.

It's disgusting, that's for sure. But I also find myself shaking my head and laughing. Ian is a man who's used to living alone and doing his own thing.

"I was thinking of making pancakes," I call as I hear him washing his hands.

"I don't think I have any of the stuff," he says as he walks out. "I don't keep too much around here. Might find everything at Lula's though."

"To be honest, your grandmother kind of terrifies me," I admit as I start pulling out the flour and sugar and all the ingredients he does in fact have. "And the only thing I see you don't have is maple extract. Think she'd have that?"

"Not a chance in hell she doesn't," he chuckles. I don't think he's realized he's only wearing boxers. Even when he slips his shoes on and opens the door. It's *really* difficult not to enjoy the shirtless view. "I'll be back in a sec."

I smile to myself and blush as I turn back to the kitchen.

He doesn't have a mixing bowl, but I find an empty, big sour cream container that works. No measuring cups, either, so I have to eyeball everything. But when you've worked at a bakery for four years, it's not too much of a challenge. By the time Ian returns with the maple, I've already got them cooking in the same skillet I used as a shield to Ian's blow this morning.

"Thank you," I say as I take the bottle from him and start on the syrup.

"You like cooking?" he asks as he leans against the fridge and watches me.

He really should put a shirt on. Because it's really hard not to stare at those perfectly defined abs and chest muscles.

I shrug, pretending I wasn't looking. "Before I moved here, I supported myself by working in a bakery. Cooking paid the bills."

"Well, I'd offer you free rent in exchange for your skills, but you've got a much nicer place to stay when all this settles down."

I glance back at him over my shoulder and laugh. "I'd offer you free rent for your vampire deflecting skills, but I don't think you'd take me up on it. You've got others who need you."

He gives a little one-sided smile and a tiny nod.

Once breakfast is ready, we sink onto the couch. Me cross-legged, facing him, Ian with his legs stretched out and his feet on the wobbly coffee table.

"So, what's on the agenda for today?" I ask around a mouthful of sweet goodness.

"These are so much better than Lula's grits," Ian actually moans in pleasure. I just smile in pride. He swallows his bite and licks at a bit of syrup on his lip. "So, I thought we could start with some basic defensive skills. We can talk more as we do that. But I do have to take Elle into town sometime today, and I have work tonight. I've got the graveyard shift that starts at ten."

"To be honest, it kind of surprises me that you leave your family at all," I say. "No offense, but you seem a little over protective. How do you ever leave?"

He gives me a little annoyed look, but it doesn't linger. "I may always live on the edge, always ready for something, but I can't live in fear all the time. It took me a while to realize that. We have to live our lives. And besides, Elle's pretty damn dangerous, even if she doesn't look it."

"Your fluttery, soft-spoken little sister?" I challenge. "Sorry, but that's kind of hard to believe."

"Don't underestimate her," he says with a lopsided smile. Another drip of syrup clings to his lips. "You see that garden out there?"

I glance out the window. To the side of the house, on the opposite side of the driveway, is a huge garden.

"Everything in that garden is deadly poisonous. That's my sister's baby. She started it three years ago. Kind of a morbid fascination, but hell, I thought it was pretty cool. Elle is, as far as I know, the only person who's made a toxin that can paralyze and all but kill a vampire." Ian smiles, pride flowing out of him. "She's deadly with a blow dart."

"No way," I say with an awed shake of my head. "That's amazing."

Ian raises an eyebrow and nods. "So no, I don't feel too terrible about leaving the property. Now, if you're finished, lets head outside and get started."

I finish my last bite and rinse my plate off in the sink.

I slip my tennis shoes back on as Ian puts together a bag of weapons. He gets dressed, which is both a disappointment and a relief. Two minutes later, we walk outside and around back behind the cabin. I guess I should have expected all the targets that are set up on the trees, but I didn't.

"Here," Ian says after he sets the bag down and unzips it. He tosses me a wooden stake. "That yellow one there? That's a softer target, the same consistency as a body. I want you to throw it from here and see if you can stick it."

I want to say *you're kidding?* but there's no way I'm going to look weak.

The stake is heavy and about ten inches long. I hold it on one end, let out a deep breath, and let the stake fly.

It smacks the target on the right side, but bounces off and lands in the dirt.

"Here, watch me," Ian says. He shows me his throw, which of course hits right in the middle of the target and sways back and forth. "Your feet should be like this," he explains as he demonstrates. "Keep your hand like this. And throw it a hell of a lot harder."

I do as he says. This time, it sticks, just barely on the bottom edge of the target.

"There you go," he says with a small, pleased smile. "Just keep throwing those for a while until you can hit the center. I'll do the talking."

I reach into the bag for another stake.

"King Cyrus had a son and that son had seven sons of his own," Ian begins recapping. "The King killed his son when he realized how evil and power obsessed he was becoming. But five of the son's sons rebelled against the King. They thought the way their father had. They tried to start a war against him. They didn't stand a chance against the King. As punishment, Cyrus cut them off. Disowned them in the gravest sense of the word. They could no longer claim themselves as his decedents, and they were no longer royalty. See, the King at this point had had a few centuries to gain power and money. Cyrus may not have been born a king, but he'd made himself one."

I throw my fifth stake and it comes within three inches of the center.

"Nice," Ian says before continuing his story. "Two of his grandsons did not rebel, though, and King Cyrus rewarded them greatly. Power, esteem, everything a vampire cares about. He charged them and their heirs with the keeping of the world. They were the true Royal Born. All those exiled were simply Born, they meant nothing."

I release another stake, but I'm so engrossed in the story that I miss the target completely. Ian adjusts my arm.

"The King closely tracks those Born through the Royal line. He knows every single one of them. And nearly each of them is in charge of a House somewhere in the world that consists of other Born with no claim to Royalty."

I adjust my feet just a bit, let out a deep breath, and put everything I've got into this next stake. It embeds itself deeply into the center of the target.

"Again," Ian encourages. "There are, as far as we know, twenty-seven Houses and heirs throughout the world. You'd think the number would fluctuate and grow every year, but vamps have a tendency of killing each other off for one reason or another. Politics aren't much different in the supernatural world, but tempers tend to flare hotter and more deadly."

"Not that you're complaining," I say as I launch another stake.

"Not that I'm complaining when they're killing each other off," Ian chuckles. "As you can probably guess now, Silent Bend has its very own—very broken—House of Royals."

"What do you mean broken?" I ask, looking back at him.

"A House doesn't get any respect, funding, or connections if it doesn't have an actual Royal to govern it," Ian says. He twirls a stake between his fingers, much like a drummer might with their sticks. His fingers never falter the entire time. "The House here hasn't had a leader in years because the rightful heir refused to have anything to do with it."

"Henry," I breathe. Because in my gut, I just know.

"Bingo," Ian says. He launches his stake at the target and it disappears halfway into it.

"A long time ago, Henry came to Silent Bend with his brother Elijah," Ian starts back into the story that was cut off with teeth in my neck. I lost my copy of that article in the attack. "Henry had never had any interest in politics, but his brother did. Elijah brought with him a clan of his Born vampire buddies when they came to town. Both Conrath brothers established plantations, but Elijah also established a House.

"I don't know all the details," Ian says as the tosses a stake in the air and catches it again. "Really, no one does. Most are just legends and speculation and bedtime stories told to scare kids into never sneaking out of the house. But somehow Elijah was killed. After that, the House should have been Henry Conrath's, but he refused to have anything to do with it. Something you should know about daddy dearest, is that no one knew a damn thing about him. He never left his Estate, as far as I know. And the House, at least most of them, they hated Henry for abandoning them. A Royal-less House is a shamed House."

My head is already spinning. I remember the picture from the article, the one of the four bodies hanging from the tree in town. Elijah's headstone.

And I finally realize why Ian and Rath were so anxious to get me away from Henry's house. "So that's why they're going to come after me," I say as my hands settle on my hips. My palms tingle as they break out into a sweat. "I'm part of this Royal line."

"And that House is yours." Ian launches another stake before walking over to retrieve the ones stuck in the target.

"I don't want to be some queen of a tiny domain," I say, shaking my head. "I mean, everyone in the House is a Born vampire, right?"

Ian nods. "They also control a few Bitten, as well."

"No." I shake my head. "I can't rule or control, or whatever, a bunch of vampires who will probably just try to kill me."

"It's more political and complicated than that," Ian says as he hands me a crossbow. He loads an arrow into it, puts my finger on the trigger, and points to a target fifty yards away. "The House may be broken without a true Royal, but they're still limping along. Jasmine Veltora has been in charge of it for the past fifteen years. They might need you, but there's no way she's going to give control of the House to you."

"Because why the hell wouldn't it be that complicated," I breathe, just as I pull the trigger. And the arrow lands dead center in the target.

"Holy shit," Ian chuckles, his hands on his hips. "I think we found your weapon, Liv."

I laugh, looking back at him and reaching for another arrow. I figure out how to notch it. Taking aim, letting my breath out slow, I squeeze the trigger. The arrow lands right next to the first.

"It sounds like I'm going to be a pawn in a very complicated world," I say as I lower the crossbow.

"In not a great crowd," Ian says. He reaches for the crossbow and loads another arrow. He takes aim and hits the furthest target dead center. "The House manipulates the entire town. There's a reason no one goes out after dark, why the police never do anything about the attacks that happen all the time—Jasmine controls the mayor. They've got a group of willing Feeders who they've promised to turn someday. The House is running this town to hell and it won't come back any time soon."

"So what am I supposed to do?" I ask. "Just run away and never look back?"

"To hell with running," Ian says as his brows furrow and his eyes grow dark. "You go into that House with all the educated cards in your deck and you burn it clean from the inside out."

Seven

WITH THE LACK OF A cell phone since mine disappeared the night of my attack and the desperate need to stay in communication with Rath, Ian agrees to take me into town with him and Elle. But I have to ride in the back of the van, where there are no windows, and keep out of sight. As the van bumps and jostles on the dirt road into town, I'm already dreading how hot it is going to get in here waiting while they do their shopping.

After parking at the shop, Ian turns in his seat. "Try to stay out of trouble."

"I'll do my best," I say, giving him a condescending smile.

"We'll try to hurry," Elle says, looking at least sorry that I'm having to wait here.

I wave goodbye to her as they climb out. I wonder how much she knows about what's going on with me. Because Ian has never told her anything with me around. But it sounds like she's well informed about her brother's world. I guess it is her world, too, since she lives in this town.

I sit so I can see out the front window, but am still blocked by the seats. I watch the townspeople as they mill about. It's a beautiful town, old but clean. There's a lot of history here. Centuries of families living and dying and being born. Paladon, Colorado never felt like this. Some towns have a soul, even if they're dark. Silent Bend has an old soul.

It's bright outside and probably pushing ninety degrees with eighty percent humidity. It's going to take a while to get used to.

I hate this. I hate hiding, feeling like I'm prey and the predator is going to pounce regardless of how prepared I feel. Ian is well trained and looks prepared, but there's an entire House of vampires that want me. And here I am, practically just waiting for it.

Such bullshit.

The heat is already stifling and I feel a bead of sweat rolling down my back. Heat pools between my breasts. I fan my shirt around me.

Such a stupid idea. I should have just stayed back at the cabin. Like a good little prisoner.

I look back up out the window just in time to see a woman pulling on her giant dog, which is leaping and jumping at something I can't see. The woman gives one little shriek before the dog pulls her awkwardly off the curb and she goes down on her ankle. Hard.

I don't think. I just spring from the van, slamming the door closed behind me. There's no one else close by and the woman is laying awkwardly half on the curb, half on the street as her dog worriedly licks at her.

"Are you okay?" I say as I reach down for her. She grabs my hands, her own shaking. Carefully, I help her to her feet, but she doesn't put any weight on the twisted ankle.

"Stupid dog," she says with a honey smooth Southern accent. "Don't know what he thought he was going to chase after."

It's no surprise he pulled her right over. He's the biggest black Great Dane I've ever seen. I'm pretty certain he could eat me if I got on his bad side.

"Come here," I say, wrapping an arm under hers. "Let's get you to that bench."

"Thank you," she says, limping alongside me. It takes us about thirty seconds to make it the fifteen feet to the bench, and she collapses onto it as the dog licks her hand.

"I'd offer you a ride to the clinic, but I don't have a car," I offer as I sit next to her. Everything in me is itching to get back in the van and hide. And I absolutely hate that.

"Oh," she laughs at herself. "I'll be alright. Just need to give it a minute." She looks at me and offers the warmest smile.

She's a gorgeous woman. Honey brown skin. Highlighted hair that's woven into perfect soft curls. Curves all over the place. She looks like she's probably in her mid-thirties. She adjusts her sunglasses, which were knocked askew during her fall.

"I'm glad you're okay," I say with a smile. "You went down pretty hard."

The dog shifts over to me and nudges my hand.

"Sorry," she says. "He's an attention hog. He just wants you to pet him. He really is a gentle giant. Don't know what he was doing before."

I reach out and pet him hesitantly. I love dogs, but this one is intimidating. "What's his name?"

"Teddy," she laughs. "He was the runt of the litter when I got him and he reminded me of a short haired teddy bear. It just kind of stuck."

"Cute," I say, and it's kind of true.

"You must be new in town," she says, studying me with the tilt of her head. "I don't recognize you, and I know pretty much everyone in Silent Bend."

"Oh," I say. My heart has suddenly taken up residence in my throat. "I'm just visiting."

"I see," she says with a knowing smile. "You must be Elsa's cousin. She said you were coming."

"Yep," I lie, interlacing my fingers between my knees uncomfortably. "Elsa's cousin."

"That Elsa is a sweet girl," she says, crossing her legs and looking out over the quiet street. A man on the sidewalk on the other side of the road glances in our direction and then does a double take. His pace quickens.

"Uh huh," I say. My instincts kick in and I'm fighting the urge to run. I should have grabbed a stake from the van. But I'm an idiot, and I've got nothing.

"You know, in a small town like this," she continues. "You have to be careful. Everyone is always up in everyone's business and they all think they know you without knowing you. Know what I mean?"

"Yeah, I think so." My breathing has picked up and my eyes are searching the shops around us. Which one did Ian say he was going into? Can he see me right now? I'm sure not, otherwise he'd probably be flying through the streets, stake in hand, no matter who witnessed.

"'Cause you know, there's two sides to every story. Have you heard the story about the Hanging Tree?" She looks down the street to the dead tree at the end of the road. And then she looks back at me, except I can't see her eyes through the glasses.

"No, not really," I manage to get out.

"About two hundred years ago, this town was dying. There were only a few hundred people here, trying to make a living off the river shrimp. But the bugs, the swamps, and the lack of money kept people away. People weren't surviving. Things were looking bad, and people started moving away from Silent Bend. Then two brothers came to town, bringing with them all kinds of money. They started two plantations. Created jobs. Started pushing that money back into the community. The town and the people flourished, thanks to these brothers." The dog finally sits next to the woman, staring vigilant out at the passers by.

"But something strange and unexplainable happened. Something out of the brothers' control. To the town there was only one explanation. The brothers. So they came after one of them. Attacked him and killed him. Tied him up, gagged his dead body. They dragged him to that tree. And they hanged him up with three of his closest friends."

I swallow hard, looking out into the street, but not seeing any of it.

"They tried to burn the other brother alive in his home. These two brothers, whose houses had done nothing but save this town, were rewarded with death and destruction.

"So you see, you can not always believe everything you hear," she says, looking back at me. I'm at once terrified of her and wildly curious to learn more. "Especially in sleepy little towns like this one."

Suddenly she stands, and there's not a single hint of the injury she sustained earlier. No limp, no favoring. She stands tall and sure.

"It was nice to meet you, Alivia Ryan," she says with a little smile. Teddy shifts around, ready to leave. "If you ever want to hear more sides to more stories…"

She drops something on the bench. I look down at it and back up, only to find her nowhere to be seen.

On the bench, right next to me, are two envelopes. I pick them up. One is simple and on the front it reads *For when you have the time to learn some more family history.* It's thick, like there are several pages inside. I set it in my lap and turn to the other envelope. The paper is expensive, with a slight shimmer to its linen color. My name is written on the front in beautiful handwriting. I turn it and confirmation freezes in my veins.

From Jasmine Veltora and the House of Silent Bend.

I'd seen sitting with the stand-in House queen.

But she hadn't attacked. She hadn't tried to drag me off. Hadn't done anything.

There are two sides to every story.

I slide my finger along the wax seal, popping it. From the envelope, I pull a thick piece of paper.

You have been cordially invited to the House's annual Summer Founders Ball. Black-tie attire required. Saturday, August 29ᵗʰ, 9:00 PM. Town hall.

There are two sides to every story. And suddenly I'm dying to know them both.

Eight

"YOU'VE GOT ONE MORE WEEK." I tell Ian after we get back to his house that evening, just before he's about to leave to go to work. "One more week and then I'm going home."

"What are you talking about?" he asks as he finishes packing up what he needs for the night. It's not just your usual medical bag. He slipped in a handgun and five stakes. **He wears his uniform, medical patches here and there, fully looking** the part of an EMT, but with a few deadly tricks up his sleeve.

"I'm not going to hide away here for months, training to be a vampire killer, too. I'm not going to waste weeks and weeks cowering away," I say, feeling my blood boil hot. Which I know isn't fair. This is coming out of left field for Ian. But I'm tired of what isn't fair, and right now I feel like I'm standing in the middle of an ocean of it. "One week and I'm going home."

"You've adapted well to pampered life," he says coldly as he zips the bag and looks up at me. "You've spent one week at the Estate and it's already home?"

"Don't you judge me, Ian Ward," I accuse him. My eyes turn cold and hard.

"Whatever," he says, yanking his bag from the table and heading toward the door. "Rath isn't paying me enough to put up with your moods."

Without another word, he walks out the door and slams it shut behind him.

I should have figured Rath was paying Ian. Why else would he invest so much time into helping me? But for some reason, this stings.

Things are frosty between Ian and I for the next few days. He teaches me basic self-defense. He makes me exercise. A lot. I'm in shape, but I'm no athlete. We shoot. He makes me attack him, but I always end up with the bruises. I catch my chin on a sharp rock one day, and he stitches me up like it's no big deal.

But I'm a quick learner. Even Ian has to admit it.

Three days before I head home, Ian comes home from work. It was a day shift this time. His schedule is unpredictable.

"There's something weird going on," Ian says as we practice with the crossbow that evening. He wears a Hipsbro County EMT t-shirt and a scowl on his face. "Like, normal weird, for Silent Bend."

"What's that?" I ask as I fire the arrow. I love this thing. I'm just as good with it as Ian. We're practicing with the wooden arrows.

"So football is a big deal in the South, I'm sure you've figured that out," he starts. And it's true. School doesn't start until tomorrow, but everyone is already talking about the all-star high school team they're going to have this year. "And we've got this quarterback that is going to be a senior this year, Tyler Black. He's already committed to play for some big college. I mean, this kid is a star throughout the state and he's only seventeen."

"What so weird then?" I ask.

"He's been missing for three days," Ian says as he twirls a stake. It's his favorite non-thinking thing to do.

"I don't know, I guess that is kinda weird," I say as I hit the target dead center.

"The police department informed the EMTs this morning, which isn't good. And if they're telling people about it, it means the House had nothing to do with his disappearance."

So the House controls what the police do and do not look into and make public knowledge. I can see how that would be essential to a House of vampires.

"Maybe it's nothing," I say as I set the crossbow down. "I mean, kids go missing all the time for different reasons. Drugs, fights with parents, girls."

Ian shakes his head. "I don't know. After being in this town for so long, it's kind of hard to believe it would be for such a mundane reason."

"Not everything in the world is tied to the supernatural," I say, raising an eyebrow at Ian.

He looks up at me from beneath those thick eyelashes of his. "Look, I know things have been a little cold between us the last few days, but I get why you want to go home. And I'm sorry for what I said the other day. It's not like you asked for any of this."

And at his words, something instantly loosens up in my chest. I've been feeling cold and tight since our little spat, and I hate it.

"Thanks," I say quietly. "Everything's happening so fast. I'm just…trying to adapt."

He offers a small little smile. "You're doing a pretty damn good job so far."

I give him a little smile back and catch the shotgun he tosses to me.

THAT NIGHT, AFTER I'M SURE Ian's fallen asleep, I read what is in the other envelope Jasmine gave me.

It's a journal entry that was ripped from its binding. The author is unnamed, and the penmanship is sloppy. The paper is old and brittle. But the story is horrific.

This man was there the night the town attacked the Conraths.

A member of Elijah's house had fathered a child. The mother hid the child's existence for three years. Until the child died—and resurrected days later. It bit and drained its mother. In front of several witnesses.

They killed the "abomination." That's what spurned the attack.

Everything I've learned is mortifying. But worst of all is what happened after.

Henry Conrath, my father, broke. The town tried and succeeded in burning him out of his home. But he came to town. He found his dead brother hanging in the tree.

He broke.

In all, he slaughtered thirty-two people in town. Drained them. Tore their limbs from their bodies, snapped their necks.

For all to see.

And when he was done, he returned to his estate and was never seen again.

NOW I KNOW WHY HENRY'S staff look at me with fear. Now I know why so many townspeople fear the night and know about the vampires. Their descendants know what happened that night in 1875. Now I know why the few people I've talked to in this town seem afraid of me.

They know what my father did.

And they know what I might do someday.

THE EVENING BEFORE I PLAN to head back to the Estate, Ian and I jog up the driveway. He's put me through a hellish seven-mile run and only let me stop once every three miles. I'm so not a runner.

"Think you're going to puke again this time?" Ian teases as we slowly jog up the driveway. I just look over at him and flip him the bird because I'm too out of breath to say *screw you*. "That's my girl."

I don't know what he means by that, but I smile all the same. I smile even more when his shoulder bumps mine, and the back of his hand brushes against my knuckles.

It's clear there's something wrong the second the house comes into view. The front door is wide open, and everything is unnaturally quiet.

"Elle!" Ian immediately shouts and darts toward the house. Even I find an extra store of energy to sprint forward. "Lula!"

When we burst through the front door, the living room is ransacked. Lamps on the floor, pillows everywhere, broken bits of now unidentifiable objects crunch under my feet. "Elle!" Ian yells and darts toward her bedroom.

She's lying on the floor, unconscious. "Elle!" Ian yells again as he drops to her side. He's immediately checking for a pulse. Next he checks her pupils.

"Is she okay?" I ask. My throat is tight, and I'm looking over my shoulder for the attacker. My knees bend slightly, and my fingers automatically curl into fists.

"No concussion, so I don't think she was hit," he says, looking her over and slipping into EMT mode. "I'm guessing she inhaled something."

"Like chloroform?" I ask. My hands shake slightly. I've read and been told stories, and yes, I was attacked myself, but this? This is right in front of me. This is tangible and real. I'm in way over my head.

"Something like that," he says. He gathers her up in his arms and lays her gently on the bed.

"I think they got what they were looking for," I say as my eyes settle on the cabinet in the corner.

The lock is busted to hell. It's a tall cabinet, about six feet tall and three feet wide. The doors swing open, half ripped off their hinges. The top shelf contains a few random scattered vials. Glass is shattered across the carpet right below it, the carpet wet.

"Shit," Ian hisses. "Those are Elle's toxins. There were at least fifty doses in there."

"Who is ballsy enough to break into *your* house and steal something to hunt down a House of *vampires*?" I hiss quietly.

"Someone completely bat-shit crazy," Ian growls. He pulls a handgun from the drawer in Elle's nightstand and steps around me into the rest of the house.

I follow him, just as silent. Quietly, he steps into Lula's bedroom. She's snoring like an overweight hog.

"Lula," Ian says, shaking her shoulder. "Grandma."

She suddenly opens one eye, glaring death at her grandson. "What the hell you waking me up fo'?" she demands. "I was havin' a nice dream about Winston. Why you gotta' go and drag me back from that?"

"Sorry, Lula," Ian says. "You didn't hear anything in the last hour or so, did you?"

"Boy, get out of my room and let me go back to sleep." She grunts as she rolls onto her side, her back to us.

We both step outside, and Ian closes her bedroom door quietly. "Lula could sleep through a hurricane these days and still not wake up when the house came down on top of her."

Ian checks his cabin and comes back three minutes later with word that it hasn't been touched. Whoever broke in is long gone.

"Why does anyone still live in this town?" I ask as I sweep up the mess in the kitchen. "It's just chaos here, all the time."

"When your roots run deep, it's hard to walk away." He rights a chair in the living room and puts the cracked lamp back on the end table.

"I guess I just don't get it," I say, shaking my head. "It's just not like that where I come from."

"Like two different worlds," Ian says quietly.

That's for damn sure.

Nine

IT TAKES A LONG TIME for Ian to settle down enough to go to bed. He rushes into the house about every ten minutes to check on Elle. He takes his medic bag every single time. But she's going to be okay and everything is quiet.

"You should get some sleep," I tell him when it gets close to midnight.

"Yeah," he says in a scoff. "Someone attacked my family and I'm going to sleep tonight."

A yawn starts to take over and I stretch my arms over my head. "Either you try or I'm going to drug you. I'm exhausted, but you're keeping me all keyed up."

"Look, you don't have to stay up with me," he says, looking out the window again. "I'll be fine. Just go in the bedroom, shut the door, and pretend I'm not out here."

I take a step toward him and place a hand on his forearm. "Ian, everything's okay now. They're long gone, they got what they wanted. So calm down."

His eyes flicker to mine and they burn with intensity. Relaxing is something Ian never does. He's a born fighter with plenty of fuel to keep him burning hot for a long time. But there is exhaustion in his eyes.

"Okay," he says quietly.

So, as we've been doing for the past seven days, we quietly get ready for bed. We both stand at the sink brushing our teeth, and I can feel the tension and anxious anger rolling off of Ian in waves. I want to reach over and smooth out all of his angry wrinkles. I want to pull him into my arms for a minute and force him to relax. But I just keep stealing glances at him in the mirror.

We change into sleeping clothes. And at 12:31, we say goodnight.

My dreams are scattered and many. At one point my mom and I are taking a walk through the park by our old house. But then something jumps out of the shadows and she's gone. And then there is a red queen with a giant bear beside her, making demands of me that I can't understand. And there is Ian, always in the shadows, along with the hint of a man named Henry. But Henry has no face.

I roll in my sleep, tossing and turning and never at peace.

As something jumps at my face with fangs and blood, my eyes fly open.

The bedroom is dim, and it seems fuzzy and unreal as my heart pounds in my chest. The blankets are tangled around my feet, making me feel imprisoned. Sweat coats my skin, the humidity and my nightmares combining. I kick the covers off, lying exposed on the bed staring at the ceiling.

A soft snore all too close pulls my eyes to the corner.

Ian sleeps in a camping chair in the corner of the bedroom. His legs are stretched out in front of him, crossed at the ankle. A shotgun rests in his arms, pointing at the ceiling. I can see a stake poking out of his pocket.

Last I saw him, he was heading to bed on the couch.

But at some point, he snuck back in here without me hearing him. He stood guard. With a gun. Over *me,* not his sister or grandmother. Through another intended sleepless night.

I lie back down, my cheek on the pillow. I study Ian's face. The scruff that's always on his chin. His dark, heavy brows. The tight lines that are already forming around his eyes from the constant worry. His thin lips pressed together tightly, even in sleep.

The heart is a complicated thing. Ian's. Mine.

I stare at him until I fall back asleep.

I'M BOTH RELIEVED AND ANXIOUS when Ian drives me back to the Estate Wednesday morning. It looks exactly the same as it did when we left, but darker somehow, full of secrets.

Ian insists on carrying my bag up to the door, where Rath takes it. He was waiting for us.

"I work the next two days," Ian says. He lingers on the porch after Rath has taken my bag into the house. "But maybe I could come by Saturday evening and we can do some more work."

I've never been a good liar, so I do my best. I look Ian in the eye and try to breathe normal and slow. "I actually have something I need to take care of Saturday. What about Sunday?"

There's a flicker in Ian's eyes, and I already feel like I've been caught in the act. But he just nods. "Everyone will be at church Sunday morning, so we'll have the run of town to ourselves."

"You mean you're not a church goer?" I tease with the hint of a smile.

"Hey, I've got nothing against any higher power. My perspective on the big picture is just a little different than a chapel." He smiles, too. A full one that makes those smile lines form in his cheeks.

And as we say goodbye and he walks back to his van, I realize where the source of my anxiety is coming from.

It's a separation issue.

I'M ABOUT TO HEAD TO bed that night when Rath knocks on my door.

"Yeah," I call as I pull my hair up into a knot on the top of my head.

Rath opens the door just slightly and doesn't look in my direction. "There's someone here to talk to you, Miss Ryan."

"Who is it?" I ask in confusion as I walk toward the door.

"The Sheriff," Rath says. His reaction is conflicted, like he'd very much like to toss him out, but also is slightly afraid of whom I'm about to find downstairs.

The Sheriff is indeed at the bottom of the stairs, waiting for me. He takes his hat off when he sees me and gives a little tip of his head.

"Sorry to bother you, Miss Conrath," he says in his heavy Southern drawl. "But I've been tryin' to get a hold of ya for the past week. Decided to take my opportunity when I saw the lights on in the house."

"It's Ryan, actually," I correct him. We stand there uncomfortably for a moment, and I realize it's because he never tries to shake my hand.

"Miss Ryan," he says, giving an uncomfortable look. "I, uh, wanted to talk to you for a while, if you don't mind." His eyes dart up to Rath, who is standing behind me, half way up the stairs. "Alone."

"Okay." Cause what else can I say?

And when I invite the Sheriff into the library it is the first time I start to feel like this house is actually mine.

"I didn't get your name," I say as I close the door behind us.

"Luke McCoy," he answers. He wanders the library for a minute, observing it in its entirety. He stops in front of the picture of my father and studies it. So I take the opportunity to study him.

He's young for a sheriff. Thirty, maybe thirty-two. A completely shaved face shows a strong jaw line. Strong hands, strong arms. Dark eyes that reveal dark knowledge.

"You know," he says without looking away from Henry. "I became Sheriff when Jasmine killed the previous one last year. He said something or another to piss her off, and she ripped his throat out. I was standin' right there."

"I'm sorry to hear that," I say as goosebumps flash across my skin. I try to imagine it: the soft, easy-South woman I'd met with blood dripping down her mouth, murdering a human being like that.

"She may look all sweet and kind and she knows how to talk you into thinking she's the best thing that happened to this town since its creation," Luke says. "But she's a bloodthirsty killer."

He takes a few steps toward me and removes his hat again. He holds it between both hands behind his back and his eyes finally fix on me. "I'm here to ask you what kind of person you are, Miss Ryan."

"What kind of person I am?" I repeat. Because what kind of question is that?

Luke nods. "I need to know. Because I am well aware of what you father was and if you are who you and Rath say you are, I know *what* you will be someday. And I know what your heritage implies and how that might change everything in this town."

I swallow hard. Luke's eyes are intense and dark, and suddenly I'm just a little scared. If I give the wrong answer, what would he do?

"I am not a killer," I say, standing a little taller. "I am not a manipulative person. I am not a politician, and I am not a pawn."

We stare at each other for several long moments and I can feel this silent dance going on between us. The dance of truth and trust.

"I'm hoping you're also not a liar," he finally says. But I do see his eyes soften. He looks away and walks to an overstuffed chair and takes a seat.

I perch on the edge of the sofa.

"You need to be aware of how the town is going to react to your presence here," he says. "It helps that you don't go by the name Conrath, but it sure *doesn't* help how much you look like Henry."

"How many people even knew what he looked like?" I ask, feeling myself relax just slightly now that I'm not being interrogated. "I mean, as far as I can tell, he never left the Estate and hasn't been an actual part of this town since they tried to kill him in 1875."

Luke leans forward in his seat and rests his elbows on his knees. "Henry didn't come out often, but he did sometimes. Always at night, but people have a habit of peering out their windows in this town. Henry visited the Hanging Tree every year on the anniversary of his brother's death. He'd leave one white rose at the base of it. There's a reason Henry is such a legend. He was like the boogieman, and everyone was terrified of him, but incredibly eager to catch a glimpse of the immortal man. I assume you know what he did the night his brother was killed?"

I nod, swallowing hard. "I know he killed a lot of people in the town."

Luke also nods in confirmation. "It was the most quickly resolved uprising in history. For a few, brief hours, Silent Bend tried to fight against the vampires, and in just twenty minutes, Henry killed that fire. Put the fear of your species back in them tenfold."

"The vampires are not my species," I bite.

"They will be soon enough," he quips right back. Luke is a no bullshit man. "And that's why people in this town won't seem all to friendly once they know who you are."

I'm already learning that. I recall Bella at the library. The way she looked at me with fear.

"A lot of people in this town are descendants of victims of that night," Luke continues. "They know the stories. Others have just heard the legends. And others don't believe the stories that are told in the dark. Just know, you might not ever fit in in this town."

"Thanks for the warm welcome-warning," I say with slightly clenched teeth.

"I just thought you ought to know what to expect," he says as he stands and starts for the door. "I hope I can count on you being the good person you say you are. Silent Bend could use some change."

I follow him out into the foyer. "I don't know that I can bring about any change, but I do try to stay true to my word." It's hard not to take offense to his approach, but I get it.

Rath walks out of the ballroom to join us beneath the chandelier.

"You folks have a good night," Luke says as he opens the door and lets himself out.

"You too, Sheriff," I say quietly as the door closes.

Ten

SATURDAY EVENING, AT NINE O'CLOCK, I stare at myself in the full-length mirror in my massive closet.

The dress is beautiful. Strapless with a sweetheart neckline, a rope of a corset back laces me in tightly. The fabric is pale pink. Beaded throughout the chest and waist, it then explodes around my waist in folds, gathers, and poofs. It's complicated, intricate, and gorgeous.

It'd been in the attic, with an assortment of other unexpected things. Bird cages, boxes of dirt. The skeleton of what appeared to be an alligator.

I did my own hair and makeup. It was something my mother loved, and I was always her doll. I watched her, and it was a tradition every few months to doll ourselves up like we were going somewhere important and grand.

My hair twists into a complicated bun. My skin glows, my eyes dark and smoky. I shimmer and shine.

Hanging from my neck, always present now, is a silver necklace, with Henry's mystery key attached to it. I tuck it into my dress, between my breasts. Out of sight.

Grabbing my mask from the dresser in the middle of the closet, I slip my white heels on, and walk downstairs.

Rath waits for me at the bottom of the stairs, concern and disapproval all over his face.

"It surprises me that Ian agreed to let you go to the Summer Ball," he says. But always a gentleman, he extends an arm for me to take. He opens the door for me and we walk down the stairs to where he has the car parked. The Ferrari, of course. "This event has been run by the House for over fifty years."

"He thought it would be wise for me to know the individuals," I lie. "All part of my education. We're running out of time."

"And he's meeting you at town hall?" Rath says again as he opens the door for me. I nod as I slip in.

Rath takes the driver's seat, and we wind down the long driveway. We turn right toward town.

And the city is alive.

Twinkle lights are everywhere. The sidewalks are filled with people dressed in gorgeous gowns and tuxedos. For a moment, I can almost imagine we're back in 1875, before the attacks. The dresses, the out of century event we're heading to.

The people of Silent Bend don't have modern worries or cares tonight. They laugh. The live. They breathe.

It's one of the most beautiful things I've ever seen.

But I remember why I am going tonight. And how I hid like prey last week.

"So, was it needed to send me into exile?" I ask as we slowly make our way through the crowd.

Rath stares forward out the window. "Two Bitten dropped by the house the first night you were gone."

"Dropped by?" I contest, raising an eyebrow. "And what happened after that?"

"I very kindly asked them to leave the premises," he says without looking at me.

"And did they comply?" I encourage.

"No, they didn't." Not another ounce of explanation.

There's a chill to the statement that hints at what Rath did to resolve the problem. I wonder if there are two new graves on the estate grounds or if maybe Rath has his own stash of vamp eating alligators somewhere.

Once again, I find myself asking if Rath is an ordinary human, a more extreme version of Ian, or the most composed vampire in all of time. Then again, I've seen his eyes, and they appear to still dilate. From what I've been taught, that's a sure sign of still being human.

We park right in front of city hall. It's an ancient, beautiful building that nearly rivals the Conrath Estate in its historical charm.

"You call me for *anything*," Rath reinforces. His eyes are dead serious and pained. This isn't easy for him. He served my father and now that loyalty has transferred to his only daughter.

"I'll be okay," I say, resting a hand on his forearm. "I promise."

He looks like he wants to believe me, but I can tell he doesn't.

I climb out and shut the door behind me anyway.

Bodies crowd into the building, heels click on the concrete steps. Jazz music, lively and entertaining, spills out onto the sidewalk.

Twice the enchantment exists in here as did outside.

It's something from a dream. Lights and lace and candles and twirling gowns and masked faces. The party already started an hour ago. It's well under way. The scent of alcohol is heavy, woven with women's perfumes and the candles.

When the crowd surges forward from behind me, I am forced to step inside and become a part of this.

Quickly, I slip my mask on.

I'm walking into the lion's den, but I am not unprepared. There are no less than ten stakes hidden in the folds of my skirt. There's a handgun strapped around my calf. I wish I could have hidden a crossbow on me somewhere, but the dress didn't begin to allow it. My cell phone is tucked between my breasts with Rath and Ian's numbers on speed dial.

A drunken couple stumbles into my back, nearly sending me flying. I crash into a man walking by, and he catches me awkwardly.

"Whoa there," he says, smiling as he rights me. He wears a mask with a flare of peacock feathers. He gives me a devilish smile. "Did you just fall from heaven, angel? I must insist you be more careful."

I barely resist rolling my eyes.

"Save a dance for me later," he says, winking at me before walking away. I watch him as he goes. He exits out a door toward the back of the ballroom.

As I look around the room, everyone is suspicious.

The House hosts this party every year, Rath had said. I can only assume that every one of them attends their own party.

I wonder, if I weren't wearing this mask, if my face weren't hidden, how many people would recognize me for who I am? How many people here would be afraid of me? How many would look at me with disdain and condemn me for the sins of my father?

Is what he did really a sin? It was the town that attacked in the first place, after all. My father had done nothing wrong. I'm not sure how I would have reacted if I'd seen my only brother so brutally murdered and then put on display for all to see.

A waitress with the faint yellow glow in her eyes of a Bitten offers me a glass of wine. I take it without realizing what I'm doing, so I don't drink it. I need to be as clear minded as possible tonight if I'm going to survive.

Fifteen minutes pass, and finally, the crowd shifts, and I notice the nine ornate chairs at the front of the hall. Sitting in the center one is a masked Jasmine Veltora.

To her right is a black man in an ornate suit and a simple black mask. In another chair is a severe-looking young woman in a tight suit. There's another young man. And then I see the man who caught me walk back into the ballroom. He wipes at something in the corner of his mouth before taking his seat. The two are unmistakably brothers, even with the masks on.

"Awesome party, huh?"

I spin around to the voice behind me.

There's a guy there, probably a little bit younger than me. He's holding a plate with an assortment of food. His smile is bordering on comical, and I can smell weed on him. He's high as a kite and one of the perky, happy kinds. And of course, he wears a jester's mask.

"Yeah, some party," I say, looking around the crowd.

"You should try the food," he continues. "It's to die for. I am so hungry. Well, I should be so hungry."

I don't know what that's supposed to mean, but the kid turns and walks away.

I work my way further and further into the crowd. Couples surge and dance and kiss and smile and laugh. I find myself feeling caught up in it all. This is glamorous and from another time and place than the one I come from.

My view to the thrones opens up again, and I see another woman take her place. She's thin, but looks strong, with short black hair and glowing skin. And her dress is amazing.

Except for the two small red dots on her sleeve.

I try to remind myself why I'm here tonight. Why I've walked into the nest of those that are coming after me. Why I have this feeling inside of me like I have to warn them about what happened at Ian's house.

Why am I here?

Because when you're backed against the wall, you have to turn the tables and find a way to break through the wall at your back.

The song comes to an end and suddenly there's the metal screech of an unhappy microphone.

"Sorry about that." I turn to see a middle-aged man standing up on the stage with the band. He wears a suit and his mask has been pulled up on the top of his head. Crows feet stretch out from the corners of his eyes, and he smiles brightly. A beautiful woman stands beside him. "Thank you for coming out tonight," he continues. And it hits me—this man must be Mayor Jackson. "We hope you've had a wonderful time. We thank Miss Voltera for the wonderful evening." There's fear in his eyes as he raises a wine glass in her direction. When I look back at the mayor, I notice Sheriff McCoy standing just off the side of the stage, watching the party with disdain. "Enjoy this last song, and have a safe night."

The partygoers clap, happy, excited, and all too ignorant.

That is when I lock eyes with the man who caught me earlier again. He gives another coy smile and stands from his seat. My heart drops into my stomach when he starts toward me.

He touched me earlier. He's a vampire. I've caught his attention. And there's no way this can end well.

I'm so stupid. So stupid.

"How about that dance?" he says when he finally reaches me. His eyes are hungry, in multiple ways, and I just know that he wiped blood from his mouth earlier. He extends a hand out to me.

"Sorry, but she's already been claimed for this one."

I turn as heat rises inside of me.

Ian stands just behind me. He wears a tuxedo, fitted and formed to his body. His hair is styled, not its usual wild action mess. A simple mask covers his face. His shoulders are tense and his eyes are filled with death.

I swear I hear a hiss and turn to see the man behind me filled with as much hatred. His eyes flash brilliant red. And for just a second, black veins rise up on his face.

But he doesn't say a word. He turns and walks through the crowd, looking back over his shoulder three times.

I turn back to Ian. Not quite looking at me, he wraps one hand around my waist and takes my hand in his other.

"What are you doing here?" he hisses, pulling me close. His lips tickle my ear. His hand on my waist slips low and his fingers dig into my skin just a little.

The breath catches in my chest and every nerve ending in my body goes crazy. The music surges, and this night suddenly feels too big for me to breathe.

"I'm not lying down and taking a fate I didn't ask for," I manage. My fingers cling hard to Ian's shoulder. I can feel the muscles beneath his clothes tense and tighten. And suddenly, I'm back to the days at his cabin, when he'd come walking out of the shower with only a towel and I pretended not to look. I know what his bare skin looks like, and I'm craving another glimpse.

"They won't care about a show of good faith," he says. "Do you have any idea what this party is even for?"

My silence is his answer.

"They throw this party once a year and offer massive amounts of alcohol so that people won't remember the blackouts that come from being fed on."

My eyes dart to that door at the back of the room. The blood on the woman's shoulder. The blood in the corner of the man's mouth.

"They're feeding on the party attendees," I say.

Ian nods. His scratchy cheek brushes mine. "The bite numbs and makes you forget, but people tend to realize they blacked out. A party like this with this much booze, you brush it off. It's the one time a year they feed freely upon the townspeople. It's the only way to keep people from asking too many questions."

It's terrifying and horrifying, and I'm suddenly wondering if the man was asking me to dance as my turn to be fed upon.

"It's bad, but I have to do something, Ian," I breathe.

"Walking into the fire isn't the way to do it," he whispers into my ear.

I back away just slightly, just so I can look into his eyes. There's intensity there. Enough of it to melt me clean through.

"It isn't your job to protect me," I say quietly as my eyes drift down to his mouth. "I saw you that night. You were supposed to be sleeping. But you were watching over me. You can't keep doing that."

"I can't seem to help it," he says as his brows furrow.

The music starts to swell toward the end. It's the last song of the night. Everyone seems to know it. I can feel it. Surging and surging, pushing me to an unknown finish.

"I have to do this," I say. I start to step away from Ian, toward the Royals that aren't Royals. "I won't be pushed around."

"Stay," he breathes.

"I can't." I take one step back, turning away from Ian.

"Liv, don't," Ian pleads. "Just look at me." Not too gently, he pulls me back toward him.

Without warning, his mouth is on mine and his arms are around me, pulling my center to his and our bodies explode in human passion. And all the fighting and training and bantering we've been doing climaxes into something I can't explain and don't ever want to come to a conclusion.

Ian's lips part and so do mine. Even as his breath gathers to say things I can't do. "Just leave with me. Now. Just walk away."

I give him one final kiss, feeling more alive than I ever have before, yet feeling like a sinking ship. Because I know I cannot give him what he wants. I pull away.

"I have to do this, and you have to let me." A million emotions are running rampant in me and I'm not prepared to deal with a single one.

Because Ian and I have been circling one another in close orbit. We have gravitational pull on each other that can't be explained by logic and reason. And I've always known, from the moment Ian decided not to kill me, that one day we would collide.

Sometimes fate deals you the horrible and the incredible. We can't run from either.

I take a step away from him, but Ian holds onto my hand. I take another step, and millimeter by millimeter, our fingers slip apart. Then I'm gone, and Ian is still standing there in the middle of the ballroom, watching me run into the middle of a pack of wolves.

So I turn away, and I don't look back. Because if I do, I'll lose every ounce of determination I've built today.

The crowd dissipates with every step I take. People flood toward the doors, almost as if they can sense the danger they've been ignoring all night. Darkness has blanketed the town, and everyone knows not to go out after dark. Time to escape back into the safety of their homes.

But I don't flee to safety. I'm too far past that.

I step forward, and stop right in front of Jasmine.

"I'm so pleased you could join us this evening," Jasmine says with a smile from behind her mask. And I swear, her teeth look sharper than ever tonight. She is no longer the easygoing, soft woman who needed help with a twisted ankle. She's a queen, a ruler, a manipulator. "Aren't we pleased our honored guest has joined us?"

The other House members around her all stare me down and nod. They all return to their seats, except one. Four women, four men. My skin crawls, but I tell myself to not be afraid.

I want to turn and see if Ian is still standing there watching me. But I can't. Because if he is, I will panic.

"I need to talk to you," I say to Jasmine. At the moment, she doesn't seem too threatening. No glowing red eyes, no face covered in terrifying veins. But there's a reason for all the fear in this town, and she's in charge. "I need to warn you about something that has happened."

One of the women laughs. Really, she's a girl. She doesn't look much older than sixteen. Black, greasy-looking hair, a nose ring, she's got all the attitude of every other human teenager. "Warn us. You do understand what we are, right? Why would *we* need warning about anything?"

"Have some respect, Trinity," Jasmine says with both ice and warmth in her voice and I'm not sure how that's possible. "This is the daughter of our regional leader. If she has something to say, we will hear it."

"We should get home first," the black man says. He leans toward Jasmine when he does, but never takes his eyes off of me.

"Agreed," Jasmine says. "I suggest we retire to the House. We can talk there, and then we will have our driver take you home."

One of the two brothers, the one who did not ask me to dance, gives something between a sneer and a smile, and it chills me to wonder what he's thinking.

"Alright," I say. I'm brave. I am.

People enter the ballroom now wearing work clothes. They're here to clean up, and with the flash of yellow eyes, I realize they too are Bitten. The House members all stand and start filing toward the front doors.

I finally understand then. The Born have red eyes, the Bitten yellow.

"Where is Markov?" Jasmine asks with impatience.

"You know exactly where he is," the woman with the fantastic dress says with annoyance in her voice.

With a sigh, Jasmine breaks off toward that back door. For an unknown, stupid reason, I follow her.

She opens the door.

Inside, the floor is covered in splatters and smears of red. A man stands, frozen and half limp while a man in a gray suit attacks his neck.

"Markov!" Jasmine snaps. "The evening is over. Let the man go before you turn him."

The man in the suit snaps away from the bloodied neck. His face is covered in blood, but beneath that, I see black veins rising all over his face, his eyes dark. His glowing eyes snap to me and turn wild.

"No," Jasmine says, her tone rising only slightly. "You don't get to touch Miss Ryan. And look at this mess you've made."

The man has absolutely no regrets on his bloody face. "He made for a delicious meal." His accent is heavily British.

"Time to go." Jasmine sounds increasingly annoyed. But without waiting for him, she turns and walks toward the doors. I hurry to keep up with her, not about to be left with this psychopath for even one second.

Eleven

OUTSIDE, SEEMINGLY WAITING FOR US, are three limos. Two are already full, so I have no choice but to ride with Jasmine and Markov.

"I really am glad that you have joined us tonight," Jasmine says with a smile once we've started driving. She takes her mask off. "I'm afraid that there's been a lot of unneeded fear created, and I worry over what you've been told."

"You said there were two sides to every story," I say, folding my hands on my lap, even though what I'm really doing is resting my hands on the most easily accessible stake hidden in my dress. "I'm just making sure I get both sides."

"You're a smart woman, Alivia Conrath," Markov says as he takes a handkerchief from his pocket and attempts to clean the blood from his face. His eyes no longer glow. Jasmine smiles and crosses her legs and stretches her arms across the back of her seat.

"It's Ryan," I correct Markov. "I've never been a Conrath."

"Fair enough," Jasmine concedes.

"You may have never claimed the name," Markov interjects. "But the blood runs through your veins, nonetheless."

"It's true," I agree. "It seems that family and blood are everything here."

"Here, families are not always born of blood, but earned through blood," Markov says darkly.

"Now, now, Markov," Jasmine chides. "Let's not scare the poor woman."

"How old are you?" Markov asks, ignoring Jasmine's invitation to be quiet.

I hesitate in answering, not eager to give too many details away. I have to play this situation with my cards held close. "Twenty-two," I respond because I can't think of how it can hurt me.

"Time is ticking."

And I'm afraid I know exactly what he's saying.

We drive for ten minutes and pull onto a dirt driveway, much like Ian's. The air smells murky and wet. We're back in swamp territory. I look out the front window. The moon shines bright and full behind what looks to be another plantation style house.

Elijah Conrath's home. Before he was killed.

"I thought this was once a plantation," I say as I observe the standing water and the decrepit trees rising from the muck. "Now it's a swamp. How did that happen?"

"Curses are one of those things not only found in fairytales and horror stories," Markov says.

"You mean witches are real, too?" I ask. I'm calm on the outside, but internally, I'm freaking out. I've barely gotten my head around vampires—I think witches might send me over the edge.

"If they are, they've kept themselves entirely hidden for all of time," Jasmine says. "Witches, the universe, karma. There is something out there and it has a wicked sense of justice."

This is an entire story, huge and complicated, but we're almost to the House, and my attention is focused to it.

As we pull closer, I see that this house is not like my own.

The white paint is peeling and falling from the walls and pillars. A tree looks like it has taken over the north side of the building. There are branches poking into several broken windows. The porch looks like it is sagging and half ready to collapse. Black streaks lick here and there, evidence of the fire that happened more than a century ago.

The House is shameful in more than one way.

The limos park in the front, the doors open, and the vampires file out.

Someone opens the grand but dirty front door. The entry was once majestic, but the marble floor is cracked in multiple places. The chandelier is missing crystals. And the entire place is dark because the windows have been covered. Soft lamps glow here and there, and I'm sure they're lit for my benefit.

Two attendants stand in the entryway and take masks and jackets as the House members hand them off. In this House, I'm sure they are not just human. Bitten, no doubt.

We file into a library, one similar to Henry's, but with half the books and only half the shelves still in tact. The place looks like it survived a hurricane and was only partially cleaned up after the storm.

"Welcome to the House," Jasmine says. Just like a queen, she settles into a grand, yet comfortable-looking chair. Her skirts billow around her, and Teddy wanders over to sit next to her. All she's missing is a crown. I don't doubt she has one somewhere. "It might not look like much, but it's ours."

"It's…lovely," I say. I sit on a chair and watch as all eight members stand or sit around the room.

"We all know your name, so it seems only fair that you know ours," she continues. "This is Micah Washington," she says, indicating the man who hovered so close to her all night. He stares at me with coldness in his eyes. "You spoke with Trinity Dalton." The nose-ring girl. "And Markov, obviously."

A smile forms on his wrinkly face and he winks at me. I'd never even considered that there would be old vampires, but you resurrect at whatever age you die. Markov has to be at least seventy and totally cruel and bloodthirsty.

"These are the Kask brothers, Christian and Samuel," Jasmine continues. It was Samuel who had asked me to dance. He smiles at me and gives a total *how you doin'?* nod. He sits close to me, uncomfortably so. Christian has a coy smile on his face like he'd love nothing more than to drain me dry. "And Anna Burke." The woman in the suit nods to me without a smile. She looks like she could rip anyone limb from limb without even breathing hard.

"This is Lillian Summers," Jasmine introduces the beautiful woman with the short hair and the incredible dress. "And Cameron Miller."

The stoner kid who told me how hungry he should be. Huh. He's a surprise. More like a druggy than a vampire.

Nine Born vampires.

One me.

Trinity gives a strong sniff, and when I look at her, she's staring hungrily at me with glowing eyes. "She's got a scratch on her left ankle," she says. "You smell damn delicious."

"Trinity!" Lillian barks, a look of horror on her face. "Alivia is royalty, not a midnight snack."

"She may be a princess, but right now she smells like a human blood bag." A threatening smile curls on Trinity's face. She may be a teenager, but she is also a blood-crazed vampire.

"Do you need to leave?" Jasmine asks, cold and calm. Trinity's eyes jump to hers, and the glow dies from her eyes.

Trinity looks down at the ground and doesn't say another word.

"We are sorry for all the secrecy that's been going on," Jasmine says. She's annoyed at the behavior of one of her subjects, but she takes back control. "We've been eager to talk with you since we heard of the attack and Henry's death. Our species can be a little overzealous at times."

"And that's why you sent two Bitten to my house to drag me here?" The words snap out of me before I can think about them.

There's a collective intake of breath. But no one kills me instantly for speaking harsher than I should have.

Jasmine gives a slightly ticked off chuckle. "We don't often just pick up the phone and invite people over for afternoon tea."

"Well, give that a try next time." I try to sound light, like I'm comfortable enough to make a joke. Lillian and Samuel offer a smile. Cameron snickers like it was the most hilarious thing ever.

"I will keep that in mind," Jasmine says.

My heart is beating faster and faster, and I hate that they can all probably hear it racing. They can probably smell the sweat on my palms. See my chest rising and falling just a bit too fast. I can pretend I'm brave and unafraid all I like, but they know the truth.

"How much do you know about the King and how a Born House works?" she moves on. Teddy nudges her hand and she pets his head absentmindedly.

"I know the King had two loyal grandsons and he gave them everything," I recount. "He gave them leadership of the world. Their direct descendants rule different areas."

"Good," Jasmine says. "Ian Ward didn't fill your head entirely with half-truths. And you know that your father, Henry, was a Royal Born who abandoned us."

I swallow hard. We're getting to the meat of my fear. I nod.

"You don't need to be so scared, love," she says with a smile, but the glimmer in her eyes says she's got me exactly where she wants me. "I promise you no harm will come to you while you are in my House."

Her House.

Let her keep it.

"I don't want to take anything from you," I blurt out. "I'm not a vampire, and I don't exactly feel like a princess, so I'd like to just keep living my life as normal."

Markov chuckles and shakes his head at my ignorance. Micah stares death at me. He hates me, I can feel it; and he knows nothing about me. Nothing, yet he knows as much about me as I do, I suppose.

"That's good to hear," Jasmine says, her voice once again sweet. "Because I do love this House and don't want to lose it. But we do need you."

"You know what will happen if we claim her and take her public," Micah hisses. "The King will come as soon as we do."

"And why are you so afraid, Micah?" Jasmine cuts back. "Are you afraid you won't survive his visit?"

"It is not me I worry over," he says, his voice dropping as everyone looks at him. "But you know how the King loves his games."

"He does, indeed," Markov agrees in that low voice. Even his eyes are drawn inward and dark.

"I have ruled a shamed House for fifteen years," Jasmine says. Her voice is calm and low. She is fire and ice. Calm and collected one moment, exploding with vengeance the next. There's a reason she rules this House. "I have born the shame of abandonment long enough. I will take the risk of the King's games to gain our respect."

"What does it matter if you have a Royal?" I ask. Because truly, I don't understand that part yet.

"Without you and your blood, we get none of the Royal inheritance," Anna says. It's the first time she's spoken, and she sounds just as harsh as she looks. "The Royal family supports every House throughout the world. They've had thousands of years to earn money, and they use it to keep their influence throughout the world strong through the Houses. It also is a line to all the other Houses, creating allies, sometimes enemies. Without a Royal, we are cut off from all of that. We are in a form of exile, you could say."

"Basically, we really need you or we're just a bunch of outcasts," Cameron sums up as he munches on a bag of chips. He's always eating, yet he's a beanpole.

"Where are all these other Houses located?" I ask. And it's surprising that I haven't thought to ask until now. But I remember Ian saying there were twenty-seven Houses.

Jasmine waves her hand to a map on the far wall. It's a map of the world, an old, torn, and wrinkled one. There are large pins stuck in various places. One here in Mississippi. Others that look close to Las Vegas, New York, Seattle. Several in China, Russia. South America. They're scattered across the globe. And all ruled by descendants of King Cyrus.

"Will the King just come and make sure I'm actually of the Royal bloodline once you claim me?" I ask. I'm trying to keep my head from spinning out of control with all the information.

"He will do far more than that, my love. He will want to check and see if you are his resurrected Queen," Markov says with that coy, thin-lipped smile.

"What is that supposed to mean?"

I look around to all the faces that surround me, expecting this to be some kind of joke that I don't get. Because I don't. But no one is smiling.

"After the King turned himself into the genesis vampire," Lillian says. There's a darkness in her eyes that extends beyond this story.

"He forced his concoction on his wife, as well, not knowing she was with child. He cursed himself then and her, too, in a way. He thought they could be together forever.

"They both craved blood and frequently fed," she tells. "But after only eighty-nine years of immortality together, Sevan seemed to grow ill. She was constantly hungry. She drank and drank and it was never enough. She was withering before the King's eyes. And after only a few weeks of this, she died."

"But I thought the Born were supposed to be immortal," I say, trying to keep everything straight.

"The King and his Queen were not Born, though," Christian interjects. "They are the genesis of vampirism."

"And as Lillian said, the King and Queen were cursed when he changed his wife against her will," Markov picks up the story. "The Queen died. And the King mourned her for fifty-one years. But one day, one of the King's great-great-granddaughters died and resurrected."

"The longer she was awake after resurrecting, the more she started to remember from her previous life," Jasmine takes over. "She was the Queen, resurrected in the literal sense of the word. New body, new face. But it was her. And the King had his Queen back.

"But every so often, after inconsistent amounts of time, the Queen would once again wither and starve and die. She would be gone for unpredictable stretches of time and then eventually be reborn somewhere in the Royal line."

"That's why the King keeps such close tabs on his posterity," I conclude.

Jasmine nods.

"How long has the Queen been gone for this time?" I ask. It's creepy and dark, but I can't help but feel sorry for the King. To keep losing his love like that, to not even know her face. It really is a curse.

"Two hundred and seventy-one years," Markov says.

"So the King…" I trail off, trying to put the pieces in all the right places. "Once the King hears about me, he's going to come here and see if I'm this reborn Queen."

Most of them nod, looking at me expectantly like I'm missing something important.

And then it hits me.

"But he won't know if it's me until I resurrect," I say quietly. "As a vampire."

"And he'll do it himself," Anna says softly.

The King will come here and kill me. I'll come back. But he'll kill me.

Welcome to the House of Royals.

Twelve

THEY ALL BREAK OUT INTO opinions and debates and shouts. I can't distinguish one from the other, but there's fear and anger roiling through the room. It's overwhelming and terrifying.

"Enough!" Jasmine bellows. She shoots to her feet, commanding the room in an instant and her eyes flare red. Every one of them falls silent and their eyes turn to her. "Alivia will have to make choices soon enough. She has a fate over her head that no one can stop. When the time comes, it will come. But for now, she's come to us with a warning, she says."

And I feel every one of their eyes shift to me, heavy and hot. I can't look around at them all, I'm too scared. I can't deny that. They are giants, and I am a tiny ant. So I just look at Jasmine. "You want me to tell you in front of everyone?"

Once again, Jasmine's eyes grow soft and kind. The woman is hot and cold. A small smile plays on her lips. "My child, whatever warning you feel inclined to give me should be a warning for the whole House. These people are my family."

Family. I never knew such a word could be so complicated.

I swallow once.

"I have to protect certain identities," I start. "You have to let me do that, or I can't say anything else."

The look in Jasmine's eyes tells me that she doesn't like this. She isn't used to bargaining and giving leeway. But this is a game of politics right now, and we *both* have to step carefully. "Alright. Proceed."

My heart is threatening to beat clean out of my chest. I wipe my palms on my skirts. "There's someone here in town who can make a toxin that is supposed to be poisonous to vampires."

"We know about the toxin," Markov says.

"It doesn't feel good," Cameron says, shaking his head. "Feels like death, a swift kick to the balls, a thousand volts of electricity all at the same time, and knocks you out for twelve hours."

"Sadly, yes, we've had experience with the toxin," Jasmine says.

I nod. "An entire cabinet of it was stolen from the maker just a few days ago. No traces of who took it, but mass amounts are gone."

If I'm going to survive this new world I've been thrust into, I need to earn some allegiance points. I need a chance at loyalty and trust from these people who are currently more powerful than me.

Collectively, everyone falls silent for the count of five breaths.

Then there's shouting and noise again.

No one notices when Jasmine stands and crosses the room to me. She takes my arm roughly and drags me to one corner of the room.

"How much of the toxin are we talking, exactly?" she demands. And I see the tips of her fangs extend behind her lips. The hint of red flares in her eyes.

I shake my head, trying not to tremble in fear. "I don't know, I never saw how much was in the cabinet before. I only saw the aftermath of the raid. But probably fifty doses."

Jasmine swears under her breath. Her eyes draw inward, and I can tell she's mulling over how to deal with this threat. "And you have no idea who took it?"

I shake my head again.

She takes a few moments before she speaks again. "Thank you for warning us," she says. And she means it, I can tell. "I really am sorry for all the fear that is happening right now. I know you didn't ask for any of this. It will not go unnoticed that you risked much by warning us—"

Glass shatters and wood splinters bullet throughout the room. Two figures with yellow eyes explode through the boarded up window.

They both blow into something and it takes some time before I realize that they're blow darts. Needles fly through the air, missing most, but Trinity gets caught in the leg and instantly collapses to the floor in spasms.

It was a man, a boy really, and a woman who broke into the House. And as soon as Trinity goes down, the woman flies at her, stake in hand. But Markov is already in the air. They collide. And his teeth sink into the woman's neck. There's a sick, wet shredding sound.

The boy leaps at Christian, and the two go down on the ground.

And I get to see, for the first time, real fangs. Long, extended, deadly sharp.

Every one of the House members has exposed teeth. Extended fangs are bared, and they all leap at the intruders with glowing red eyes. Everyone moves at impossible speeds, no more than a blur. Christian lifts the boy like he weighs nothing, pinning him against the wall.

I look back at Markov and the woman when there's a snapping sound. There's blood everywhere, and her arm now lies three feet from her body. He attacks her neck again, wrapping one arm and hand around her head as she frantically tries to escape. With a sickening snap, he rips her head clean off.

She flops limp to the floor and blood spills out of her wrecked body like a river.

Markov licks his lips with a smile on his bloody face.

I turn back, just in time to see a needle embed itself into Christian's neck. He collapses back into Anna and Micah. Not wasting a second, the boy darts back for the window.

He pauses, just for a second, looking back at us with those yellow eyes. And I see something on the back of his hand. A red and angry burn—a brand. It's the shape of a snake eating its own tail.

"Don't let him escape!" Jasmine screams when the boy leaps from the window. With animalistic growls and hisses, Anna and Micah both fly after him into the night.

"Let's get them to their rooms," Jasmine commands.

There's blood smeared all over the library, broken glass and slivers of wood line the floor. At least a dozen needles are embedded into walls and books, and roll around the floor.

The intruders had to have used up nearly a quarter of their stash in this attack, and they took down two members.

I realize something. There's no point in simply immobilizing House members and putting them through a couple of hellish hours. You only immobilize a vampire to try and kill them.

Markov scoops Trinity up in his arms. She's still twitching and spasming. Her eyes are screwed shut, and her teeth clench tightly. She hisses in pain. Samuel slings Christian over his shoulders. They exit the library.

"Get these needles taken care of," Jasmine commands Cameron. "Carefully."

He actually looks scared, but I see the terror in his eyes is directed at Trinity who is disappearing down the hallway. He's worried about her. But he does as Jasmine says and starts collecting the needles.

Lillian squats by the woman, her hands on either side of the dismembered head. She studies her face. "I don't recognize her. She isn't from Silent Bend."

My stomach turns at all the blood. It's everywhere, seeping down into the floorboards, running in a river toward the door, in a giant pool under the dismembered body.

When my eyes shift to the severed arm, the symbol catches my attention.

"Does the snake mean anything to you?" I ask.

"Snake?" Jasmine asks.

I point to the arm, specifically, at the back of the hand. There, branded into the skin, is the same symbol of the snake eating its own tail.

Jasmine grabs the arm, which is all kinds of disturbing, and observes the brand.

"The boy who escaped, I saw the same symbol on the back of his hand," I say. I want to go home, but suddenly, nowhere seems safe. Even a house full of Born just got broken into by a couple of Bitten.

"You're sure?" Jasmine demands, looking sternly at me.

I nod.

"We'd be able to ask about this exact kind of thing if we had any Royal connections," Lillian says. Not in defiance, just as a fact. "The Royals are a worldwide network. I'm sure they would know something about this."

Jasmine doesn't look happy about the statement, but she doesn't make a fuss. "Eventually, we will have that ability. But we're resourceful. We will find out who did this."

I shuffle into the corner of the library, feeling overwhelmed. I want to disappear. I want to go back to last month when I had no clue this dark world existed. When all I did was worry if my dough would rise right and knew that it would.

Life was so simple.

"Henry was attacked, too," I say quietly. "That's how he was killed. Rath was incredibly surprised by it. It seemed random, as well. But I don't think it was."

Everyone is quiet for a moment. What I've just said, it means something. Something heavy and future-altering.

"Thank you for the warning, Alivia," Jasmine says quietly. "I think you should go home now. We will talk more later."

And just like that, I am released.

Without a word, I turn and walk out of the library. It's quiet in the entryway. Only a few bloody footprints lead back into the mansion. But everything else looks in place and natural. I put my hand on the rusty doorknob and pull it open.

Outside, there is one limo left, as if it's been waiting for me this whole time.

Just as I'm about to climb inside, I see one figure racing back toward the house. Anna slows yards from me, heat and anger bright in her red eyes.

"Did you catch him?" I manage to ask.

She shakes her head as the glow starts to fade away. "I've never seen anyone be able to disappear like that. No smell, no traces. Just gone." Her nostrils flare, her eyes wild. Anna isn't one to be bested often. "Micah is insistent he'll find him, but…" She shakes her head. "He's gone."

"I'm sorry for what Trinity and Christian are going through," I say, and I mean it. It's not a deep sympathy because well, Trinity would have probably gladly drained me earlier, but that toxin can't be pleasant.

Anna nods her head. "You should go home now."

I nod as well. And without another word, I climb into the limo. The driver doesn't even look back at me as he pulls around in the driveway and heads out to the main road.

I'm numb and empty as we drive home.

I thought Ian had trained me enough, prepared me. All I was expecting was manipulation and forceful persuasion. I didn't expect this. Attacks and death and so, so much blood. This is so much more.

We roll up the driveway to the Conrath Estate. And I'm not surprised one bit when I see the figure sitting on the top step.

I climb out and close the door behind me. The limo takes off without hesitation.

In a movie, Ian would probably launch himself off the steps, gather me in his arms, and we'd look beautiful and lovely clinging to each other in this gown and that tux. We'd be so happy and relieved that the other is safe that words wouldn't be needed to fix the choices that have been made.

But he just sits there. With anger and fear in his eyes. And I simply, numbly walk up the stairs and sit next to him.

"You're alive," he observes.

"I'm alive."

"You got blood all over your dress," he says without looking at me.

I look down. There is blood coating the bottom of the dress, swept up from the library floor. There are also splatters of it here and there all over me. Markov is messy and crazy.

"Shit," Ian hisses, life sparking back inside of him. "Is that one of Elle's needles?" And he plucks one from my skirt. I didn't even notice it there, embedded into the folds of my dress. "Liv, what happened?"

So I tell him. All of it. The story they told me, what would happen if the King came to Silent Bend. How I warned them all. And the attack.

"I've never heard of the snake symbol," Ian says, shaking his head. "Some families adopt symbols. Family crests. Yours is the raven. But I've never heard of the snake."

"That boy," I say when something tickles the back of my brain. "The football player you said went missing. What did he look like?"

Ian digs into his pocket and brings out his cell phone. He takes a few seconds and then hands it to me.

"It's him," I immediately say. The dark, teenager-pocked skin. The almond shaped eyes. The full lips. "He's one of the two that broke into the House."

Ian nods. Like it's not a surprise at all that a missing football star turns up as a Bitten vampire. "Something's happening. Three Bitten not under control of the House. Four if you count the one who killed Henry. A very specific attack on the House. You know what that attack was?"

I shake my head. "What?"

"A declaration of war," Ian says ominously.

"By who?"

"Don't know yet."

The crickets chirp, and off in the distance, I see lightning bugs dancing through the trees. The scent of the magnolias and the wisteria floats through the air.

Mississippi is beautiful. It's old and charming and deep as it is South. But it has opened my eyes in ways I wish they could have stayed shut.

"I don't want to be afraid of all of this," I breathe quietly. I'm not sure Ian can hear it, and the statement was meant for me more than him.

"You should be afraid of this," he admits. And in a surprising show of understanding, he reaches over and puts a hand on my knee.

I shake my head. "I don't want to be afraid of all of this," I repeat, my voice still quiet. "But tonight I am and I think it's a good thing that I am."

And with the admission, all my insides begin to tremble. The shakes work their way from my insides out. Ian wraps an arm around me and gathers me into his side. My head settles into the space between his cheek and his shoulder and he crushes me to him. I cling to him.

Here it is.

I will give myself this night. I will embrace the fear and the immense new world I've been shot into. I will let everything that's happened in the last three weeks sink into my heart and shake it with everything that it is. If tears want to come, I will let them come.

Tonight I will be afraid.

But come morning, when the sun rises, when I can walk out into it and feel that, for now, I am human, I will dominate that fear.

I will embrace it all, and I will win.

Thirteen

THERE'S SOMETHING ABOUT THE PAINTING in Henry's —my—bedroom. It's a huge, nearly floor-to-ceiling masterpiece of a village with a river that runs through it. A still life, I suppose, a landscape? There are no people in it. Just the buildings, old, ancient. There's a small boat tied to the side of the canal. But it isn't the lack of life in the painting that's bothering me.

It's how it seems off. Not quite set right on the wall. Like it's just barely angled away from it on the left side.

When I woke in the morning, I did feel better. But I just laid in my bed long after the sun came up, just being. Not really thinking. Not really feeling. Just existing.

I hadn't really realized my eyes were fixed on the painting until I started to feel annoyed with it. And eventually I realized it wasn't the painting itself that I was annoyed with.

Climbing out of bed, I pad over the wooden floors to it. Preparing myself for the heaviness it must weigh, I grab either side of the frame to straighten it.

But the second I touch that left side, it swings just slightly toward me.

All the blood in my body falls to my feet as a cold draft wafts out from behind the painting.

I pull on the left side, swinging the door wide open.

Behind the painting lies the opening of a narrow passageway.

The walls are lined with old wood and stone. There's no light to lead the way, but what little spills in from my bedroom shows that it cuts sharply to the left and then drops.

The discovery of a hidden passageway is amazing. It's every little kid's dream. But I know the history of this house and what lurks in the dark in this town. I'm both fascinated and petrified about where this passage leads to.

I grab my cell phone and turn the flash on for a light. With the cold air licking over my body, I start into the dark.

It does indeed cut immediately to my left. This wall is an outside one, with windows looking out over the river just to the side of it. It's impressive there's room enough to house the passage. It runs for two yards, and immediately drops down into a set of steep stairs.

Down, down, down I go. The darkness makes the stairway seem longer than I think it actually is. The air grows cooler, the moisture in the walls thicker.

I level out into a tunnel.

Dirt walls, dirt floor, and dirt ceiling make me fairly sure that I'm underground. Wooden beams brace the tunnel every ten feet or so, but they don't look particularly stable, like they're beginning to rot out.

When I suddenly step in a shallow puddle, I understand why.

I'm probably ten feet underground. This secret tunnel is not far from the river at all. I'd bet it floods in the winter and spring when the rains raise the level of the river.

I walk and walk. It feels like forever. A mile? Two? Maybe it's only been a hundred yards, but in the dark, knowing how unstable this tunnel is, it feels ominous and unending.

And then I see another set of stairs, leading up, and a sliver of light.

A small wooden door covers the entrance. I have to push and shove. The sound of branches and leaves scrape from the other side, before I finally burst out and into the thorny shrubbery that waits for me.

The doorway is well hidden between two ancient and huge trees with thick underbrush growing around it. I tumble out, scraping my arm on a branch.

Climbing to my feet, I brush myself off and look around at where I am.

The fence, which serves as the border of the Conrath property, is directly behind the trees I climbed out from beneath. The tunnel leads directly from the Estate, which I can barely make out in the distance, to just outside the property line.

There's an empty field dotted with trees between where I am and where I can see the next houses, closer to downtown, and me.

I look back down at the entryway and something carved into the still open door catches my eye.

Elijah Conrath. March 3, 1651—October 13, 1875.

Finally, rest in peace, my brother.

Beneath the words is the shape of a raven.

I trace my fingers over the roughly carved letters. It's a reverent motion. On hallowed ground.

This is how Henry escaped the night the town tried to kill him. He probably would have been killed if he hadn't had this escape route. From here, he'd gone into town, maybe tried to save his brother, only to find him dead and hanging from a tree.

At some point, he'd carved this into the old and weathered wood.

I can feel him here. Henry. My father. At some point, he'd been here, too. Alone. Scared. Angry. Feeling like the world is unfair.

"I wish you were here with me," I say quietly into the morning light.

THE NEXT WEEK IS ONE without news or pressure from the House. Which is a relief. It allows me to get myself together. If I'm going to conquer my fear of vampires, I need to understand everything about them. I grill Rath.

The Born love blood, but they are not ruled by uncontrollable bloodlust like the Bitten, who drink blood out of obsession. Without regular drinking, the Bitten will wither and age at a much faster rate. The Born don't need more than one feeding a week. But every so often, they can snap in bloodlust.

They both eat normal food.

All vampires need sleep. The Bitten sleep just the same as humans, just usually during the day since their eyes cannot handle the light. The Born suffer from a form of "insomnia," as Rath put it. A Born's senses are extremely heightened. Their vision, their hearing, smell, touch, everything. As is their brain activity. So letting themselves relax enough to sleep is often difficult.

Vampires are predators, specifically nocturnal ones. I guess this is where the bat legend comes from. There's a lot of speculation that the King used something from them in his creation. Vampires eyes are designed, like night creatures, to dilate fully so they can see better at night. And like a bat, their enhanced sense of sound helps them see at night. But their eyes stay dilated all the time, causing them extreme discomfort and pain in too much light.

Thus, they all prefer the night.

The Born are better than the Bitten in every way. They're stronger, have better senses. Not to mention the immortal versus the aging problem. Bitten also suffer from the Debt.

When a human is bitten by a vampire and turned, a sire bond of sorts is formed. The newly Bitten feels a sense of loyalty toward the vampire who created them. They'll do just about anything for them and never once question a request.

Eventually, the Debt wears off. The length of time is never consistent. Sometimes it's only a month, sometimes it lasts for years.

The Bitten can create other Bitten vampires.

In the world, there are probably more Bitten than Born. It is easy to create more Bitten, so long as you have the right amount of self-control. But conception of the Born doesn't happen very often.

Still, the Born rule over and dominate the Bitten because they are in control of themselves. They are clear minded. And they hold the power.

And the Bitten often *hate* the Born.

It's something that fascinates me. I cannot help but feel sorry for the Bitten. I imagine many didn't ask for this life. They're changed, cursed in craving the blood of what they once were. They have to say goodbye to the sun. And then they are so often enslaved.

It sounds like a civil war waiting to happen to me.

The physiology of a vampire is not much different than a human's. They bleed. Their hearts still beat. But they all have retractable fangs, much like a cat's retractable claws. And they all produce that toxin that numbs, erases memory, and possibly turns.

I'm learning. This will be my life someday. And I must educate myself.

I stare at the painting of my father in the library, turning the key around my neck over and over.

I still haven't discovered what it opens.

Henry Conrath's eyes are dark and deep. They're the kind of eyes that lock things away, but reflect the darkness of their contents. I've asked Rath many times how old he was, but his answers are always vague. From Jasmine's story, though, I know he was at least two hundred years old. Probably older. Elijah was born in 1651, Henry could be far older or far younger.

I try to imagine someone breaking into the Estate. They crept through the halls of the house with a stake, maybe crossbow, in hand. They found my father that morning, trying to fall asleep. Henry should have felt safe in his own home in a town where everyone feared him.

But someone drove a stake through his heart. And to make it so much worse, they drug his body out into the sun to make his anguish all the more intense.

I just can't bring myself to believe the story.

Because this man that I'm looking at, he is immortal. This is a man who survived a brutal attack by dozens of people. A fire. This man killed dozens of people in less than an hour.

I can't imagine him being dead.

Even though I've never once met him.

But Rath says he is, and the sadness in his eyes tells me it's true.

Loyalty runs deeper than blood, and Rath was loyal to my father. I will never question that.

"One thing you should know about daddy dearest is that no one knew a damn thing about him." Ian had told me that early on, and it's inexplicably true.

"Who are you?" I whisper to him.

I'm about to turn away when something I'd never noticed before catches my eye. The form of a raven is painted subtly into the black of his suit jacket.

I hold the key head up, comparing them. It's the exact same raven, wings folded up, about to beat down in flight. Claws outstretched as if to grab something. Every detail is the same.

The raven is the symbol of the house of Conrath. That evidence is everywhere throughout the very house.

But this is more than just marking your possessions with a symbol—this is an obsession.

I loop the chain around my neck once again and let the key fall to my chest.

My father wanted me to have this key, and there was a reason for that. I don't know if this is a test or a puzzle, but I will figure it out.

My eyes shift from the portrait to the shelf just to the left of it.

There are four glass jars sitting there, filled with some kind of gray dust. I trace my fingers down one slowly.

And realize that it's not dust, and these aren't jars.

They're urns.

"And who were you four?" I breathe.

There are so many mysteries to my father and this house. I wonder if I'll ever unlock them all.

I walk out onto the back veranda and watch as the sun makes its way toward the horizon. The day is hot, humid in the worst way. My clothes stick to my body.

I need some stress relief, and no one is around. The staff has gone back home for the night. Rath is taking care of business, which he always seems to be doing, even though I have no idea what his business actually is.

I have the Estate to myself.

I strip my clothes off and throw them into one of the many rocking chairs on the veranda. I stand with my toes on the edge of the pool and dive in.

The water is cool and soothing. Bubbles rise out of my nose as I propel myself through the water. I break through the surface and fold my arms over the side of the pool, looking out over the river.

I've walked the riverbank several times. It smells like nature down there, but there is something frightening about it. So wide, deep, and old. Just like everything else around here.

There are houses across the river, small in the distance. It's a whole different State over there. I've never even been in Louisiana, and I see it every day.

I've seen so little of the world.

"Nice view, huh?"

I nearly drown myself as I whip around in the water. My grip on the side of the pool slips and my head half dunks under the water.

Ian stands there in the doorway into the house. His hands half in his pockets, his feet spread wide, relaxed as can be, with a coy smile on his lips.

I swear as I clasp my hands around my breasts because there they are, and the water isn't going to hide much. "Seriously, Ian?" I scream. "I thought all you males here were supposed to be Southern gentlemen."

"I never made that claim," he says shaking his head, and still smiling with pride.

I swim to the other side of the pool, using just my legs. Finally out of his view, I hurl as much water as I can at him.

"Damn, Liv," he says with a laugh and mild annoyance in his voice. He's half soaked. It was a good wave I sent his way. "Now look what you've done."

"Serves you right, asshole," I growl at him, even though a smile is fighting its way onto my face. "Just standing there and gawking like an Neanderthal."

"How could I not?" he teases me with that wicked smile. He grabs the hem of his soaked tank and pulls it up and over his head.

My face heats, and I turn my eyes away, but not before catching the sight of his sculpted chest, the rock hard stomach.

"What are you doing?" I hiss at him, fighting off a smile.

"It's hot," he says, and I can hear the smile in his voice. "You got me all wet, and I thought I'd join you in that very refreshing water."

"Like hell you're getting in here!" I protest. But really, the thought has my insides doing all kinds of acrobatics. I just stare at the tree on the edge of the river.

Ian is quiet for a minute. And suddenly something drops in the water right next to me.

My bra and panties.

"Better?" I look up at Ian who's raising an eyebrow at me. He's wearing only his boxer briefs and a smile.

I snatch my underthings in the water and glare at him.

It only takes me a minute to get them back on, and I only feel slightly less turned-on-embarrassed once I'm covered in all the important places. The second I give him the okay, Ian cannonballs into the water.

He surfaces, flicking his hair out of his face. He needs a haircut, but it suits him. Not entirely put together—free and wild.

"You really should quit staring, Liv," he says as he swims over to me. "You're going to give me all these wild thoughts that you want something from me."

"In your dreams," I breathe, trying to tease him off and totally failing.

"Many, many times since the day I met you," he confesses with no shame. He's stopped only a foot and a half away from me. He treads water with ease, and his eyes are intense on me. "You blew me off on Sunday. And haven't answered any of my calls all week. You avoiding me?"

Water droplets cling to his lashes. His lips are wet and oh so close. Ian shifts in the water and without thinking, I move with him.

I bite my lower lip without thinking. My body is freaking out. "I had some thinking to do."

"Hmm," he says contemplatively. "So, you heard from your new friends since the ball?" he asks, whiplashing the moment.

It takes me a second to pull my thoughts from what's happening in my lower belly to the question he posed.

"Uh, no," I say. "It's been a week, but there hasn't been a single word. I'm guessing they're all still trying to decide what to do with me."

"They want to claim you," Ian says.

"But they're afraid of what will happen when the King comes," I fill in.

"I've heard the stories," Ian says as all the heat dies from his eyes, leaving me with a sense of longing. Like he waved the biggest box of chocolate in my face and then ripped it away, saying, *just kidding*. "He's got this pretty sick sense of entertainment. He visits all the Houses from time to time. He gets bored easily after living for so long. Likes to play games."

"Like what?" I ask, my brows furrowing.

"I heard he rounded up a dozen humans once," he starts. "Whoever hunted down and fed on the most of them won a million dollars. Blood and money. Two of the King's favorite things."

"Why is everyone in the House here afraid of him, though?" I ask. "If he's just brutal to the humans?"

"Because another time, he took two House members and told them whoever won that game could join his Court. It was a battle to the death, and they didn't have any choice."

"I get it," I say, shaking my head. This guy sounds a bit like Markov, just with more money and more power.

"So, yeah," Ian says. "I get why they're taking so long to come to a decision on what to do with you. It's a serious matter."

I nod absent-mindedly.

"I still think you should have waited longer to out yourself," Ian says quietly.

"They'd already found me," I say, resisting the urge to start an argument. "I'd already met Jasmine, that day we went to town. She's the one who gave me an invitation."

Ian takes a deep breath and lets it out slowly when he looks away from me.

"I'm a tough, big girl, Ian," I say. My insides are feeling complicated things. It's been a long time since anyone looked out for me. "You don't have to always try and protect me. You have no obligation to me."

"Like I said," Ian says as his eyes shift back to mine. "I can't seem to help it." He very slowly moves closer to me through the water. The small wave he sends rippling around my body makes all my nerve endings fizz to life. "You do things to me, Alivia Ryan."

"What things?" I breathe, resisting the urge to close the small distance between us. Ian is only six inches from my face, but it feels like he's miles away.

"Strange, unexplainable things." His eyes shift down to my lips and the heat in the air doubles. "You're a drug I can't get off of. I know you're going to be my worst enemy someday, but I think that's part of the reason I want you so bad. I can't have you."

My own eyes are on his lips again, and I'm trying to remember what they taste like, and suddenly, I'm feeling forgetful and need a reminder.

"Are you two completely idiotic?"

We spring apart and whip around. Rath stands on the veranda, eyes livid and wild. His hands are clenched into fists, and his chest rises and falls.

"This boy is a sworn enemy of the House, and that House is watching your every move now, Alivia," he hisses. "They know exactly where you live. They have eyes *everywhere*. And you two together puts *everyone* at risk."

"I'm…I'm…" and I was about to say I'm sorry, when I remember I'm an adult and Rath is *not* my father. I don't have to apologize to him.

"I don't care what you two do with your hormones and feelings," he spits, contradicting what he just said. "But you better do it in private where you won't be seen and get anyone killed."

"He's right," Ian admits quietly. He hoists himself out of the water and holds a hand out for me. "I know better."

I meet his eyes as I stand, our bodies only inches apart, dripping water everywhere.

"Like I said, you do inexplicable things to me," he says quietly as his eyes burn into mine.

"Get inside, it's nearly dark," Rath growls as he tosses two towels at us.

I wrap my towel around my chest, Ian around his waist, and we slip past Rath like two caught teenagers. And the second we break into the ballroom, we both burst out laughing.

"See, you didn't even need Henry, you've got Rath," Ian says as we slowly walk across the cold marble floor.

That stings a little more than it should, but still, I offer a small smile.

"I am sorry, though," Ian says, the mood having already grown more serious. "I should have thought this through some more before just showing up at your house."

"Are you really an actual enemy of the House?" I ask.

Ian lets out a loud breath. "Yeah. I mean, I've hated vampires pretty much my entire life. I've killed at least half of the Bitten they've created over the last eight or so years. They know me well and everything I do and stand for. It wouldn't be good for you if they knew about…us."

"Us, huh?" I tease him as I turn into the kitchen. "I didn't know that was a thing."

"I'm not one to adhere to labels and definitions too often," he says with that smile. "I just let the cards play as they land."

"You sure know how to win a lady over, Ian Ward," I say as I open the pantry.

"What are you doing?" he asks.

I dig through the bins and shelves. The pantry in this house is bigger than my bedroom back in Colorado. "I'm hungry, and do you know how long it's been since I baked anything?"

"Right," Ian says, taking the flour and sugar canisters I hand him. "You're Martha Stewart."

I snort at that. "Don't ever call me that again."

"Deal. I'd never want to do the things I want to do to you with Martha Stewart."

"You're bad," I chuckle as I cross to the kitchen and grab eggs from the gigantic fridge. Seriously, why do we need so much food and so much room when it's just me and Rath they're feeding? "Are you this forward with all the women you come in contact with?"

"Not exactly," Ian says as he sets the ingredients on the gigantic granite bar. "I haven't been on a 'date,'" he air quotes, "in about two years."

"Too busy slaying vamps?" I tease him as I start digging around for a mixing bowl. I find one and a stash of measuring cups.

"Something like that," he says as his eyes follow me around the kitchen.

I give him a little side smile. I double-check all my ingredients, sure I've got everything.

"There's just one thing missing," I realize. "Hang on a sec."

Except, in this giant house, running to my bedroom doesn't take just a second. I have to run through the dining room, loop around through the foyer, up the staircase, down the hall of the north wing, and finally burst into my bedroom. I snatch it off of my dresser and dart back down the stairs and skid around back into the kitchen. I have to tuck my towel back in to keep it from falling.

"How old is that thing?" Ian asks with a laugh.

I plug my old school iPod into my portable speakers on the counter. "I've had it since I was a sophomore in high school, probably," I say as I click it on and scroll through playlists. I click on the one that says "RISE THE ROOF." An old rock song starts blaring through the speakers. "I brought it with me to work every day back home. I'd put my headphones on and just…"

"Get in the zone," Ian says in a half teasing tone.

"I guess," I chuckle as I start measuring out my dry ingredients and mixing them in a bowl. "I think it started 'cause my mom always listened to music when she was cooking in the kitchen."

"You don't talk about her much," Ian says. He slides the sugar toward me when I point for it. "How'd she die?"

That familiar feeling of sadness sinks in my stomach as I remember the police call. "She was walking home from work one night. Her car was having problems and she really wasn't that far from the diner where she worked. The girl was on her phone texting, the cops said. She didn't even see mom crossing the road—or the red light."

"I'm sorry," Ian says. His voice is quiet and low and I can tell he means it. "That's pretty horrible."

I nod and crack an egg. "It was. I mean, I was nineteen. I was living on my own, so I'm sure if I'd still been at home, it would have been a whole lot worse. But still."

"Of course," he says. And I realize that Ian is one of the only people who can know what it felt like. Our parents died in different ways, but they're both dead.

"I guess we're both orphans, huh?" I say, trying to make a small smile.

Ian shrugs. "I do have Lula. What about your grandparents?"

I shake my head and tip in the vanilla. "They were pretty old when they had my mom. Grandpa died when I was like six, and Grandma died only a year later. I don't really even remember them all that much. They lived in Levan, that's where my mom grew up."

"I didn't know that," Ian says. I pass the bowl to him and the whisk. He sets to mixing all the liquids together.

I nod as I pull out a baking sheet and the parchment paper. "Yep, my mom grew up there. She got a summer job here in Silent Bend after she graduated high school. She was only here for three months, but I guess that's when she met Henry."

It's depressing, thinking that there was no love between them, no deep meaning, just one night—and they made me.

"I'm sorry you never got to meet him," Ian says as he passes the bowl back to me. "I hate vampires, but he's the only one that I ever respected. Didn't know much of anything about him, but sometimes you can just tell when someone wants to be a good person. Henry never wanted to hurt anyone. He just wanted to be left alone."

I nod. Maybe that's what my mom felt when she was around him, that he wanted to be a good person. Maybe that's why she spent a night with him and later left, not knowing what she carried.

Sometimes the past repeats itself.

"She left Mississippi at the end of the summer and headed to Colorado for school," I continue the story, trying to push away the complicated feelings I have when it comes to my father. "She wanted to be a vet and they have this amazing school. It was nearly half way through the first semester before she'd admit that she was pregnant. She quit going to school after only one semester there so she could support me."

"She sounds like a good woman," Ian says quietly.

"She was." I pour the wet and the dry together and mix in the coconut and the chocolate chunks.

"You're lucky." That tone in his voice carries a lot of weight.

"I'm sorry your parents fought so much," I say. "I can only imagine."

"It was ugly," he says. He hoists himself up onto the counter and crosses his ankles. "I think Mom had all these big dreams of what she'd do with her life. She wanted to be somebody. But then she met my dad, fell enough in love with him, married him, and got pregnant right away with me. She knew she had to take care of me and Dad, and I think she kind of resented that."

"That's awful," I say as I roll the dough into little balls. "Couldn't she do both? Follow her dreams and have a family?"

"I guess she didn't feel that way," Ian says with a shrug. "I don't think they planned on having more kids, but then Elle came along."

"I guess we're both a little broken, huh?" I say as I slide the baking sheet into the oven.

"What doesn't kill you makes you stronger, right?" he says with a sad smile.

"You're a strong person, Ian," I tell him quietly and seriously.

"So are you, Liv." I look up into his eyes and there's depth and sincerity there. There's also a tiredness that's come from always being what I just told him he was.

He slips off the counter, his thigh sliding down mine in the movement, catching my towel and dropping it to the floor. But Ian's eyes don't dip, don't search my body. They stay locked on my eyes.

Slowly, his hands rise to softly rest on my cheeks. He brushes his left thumb over my cheek. I don't think he realizes he's doing it.

"It's all very tragic, you and I," he breathes quietly. His gaze is intense and deep. "I'm the enemy of a House you won't be able to run from. I stand for what I stand for, and we can't deny what you will become one day."

I hadn't thought of it that way, but suddenly there's a sharp pain in my chest. "It'd be easier to walk away now, wouldn't it? Before this goes any further. Just call it done."

"There'd be nothing easy about it," Ian counters, shaking his head. I realize he's taken a step forward, pushing me back toward the bar. "It'd be extremely painful. But it's what should happen."

"But..." I whisper. My eyes are locked on his lips. My nerve endings are sizzling to life. There's an electric storm in my lower belly.

"But I just can't."

I don't know if it is him or me that closes the distance between our lips, but instantly it's gone. They're fierce, and demanding, and frantic. There's no distance between our bodies and my back is being pressed against the bar. Ian's center is pressed against mine and I'm sure I'm going to loose my ever-loving mind into blissful obliteration.

Skin to skin. It's a maddening, beautiful thing.

Ian's hands clamp around my hips and he hoists me up onto the counter, wedging himself between my knees.

There's no walking away from this.

Ian's lips trail from my mouth down to my neck. My head falls back with a sigh as I expose more territory for him to claim.

"We should stay away from each other," Ian growls into my skin, even as his right hand trails from my neck, down my arm, over my thigh. He wraps his fingers around my ankle.

"We're going to be enemies someday," I manage through my quickened breathing.

Ian kisses his way across my throat and then back up to my lips. "But damn, there's no time like the present."

A smile crosses my lips as they are consumed again. Ian slides me back on the counter. My butt catches something and the mixing bowl with the rest of the cookie dough goes flying to the ground. Ian places a knee on the counter, hoisting himself up, pressing my body back onto the countertop. I hit something else, and the open container of sugar crashes to the floor.

Ian places a hand next to my head to support himself and smashes an egg. But neither of us cares too much, apparently, because our lips never part. My hand is exploring the wonderland of Ian's torso, and his other hand is snaking its way around my bare back.

It's been a long, long time since I've been with a man. I've been on only a few dates since my mom died. I'm far out of practice and I'm pretty sure I shouldn't be any good at this anymore.

But Ian and I together…we are magic.

I've crossed a line before, though, and there was a price to be paid.

"Ian," I say against every instinct in my body. "I…I want to be careful."

Ian backs away from me just slightly so he can look down in my face. "I don't exactly want to stop this, cause damn," he chuckles, and I can feel all the ways his body is reacting. "But I'm not the kind of guy to just take a girl on the kitchen counter for his first time."

A little chuckle makes its way out of my chest. "There's no way you're a virgin," I say before I can think to stop it.

"And why the hell not?" he demands, his brows furrowing in offense.

"Because," I say. I can't help the smile on my face, he's totally joking. "You're you. You're all cocky and presumptuous and you say the stuff you say without thinking twice about it. There's just no way."

"Well," he says, his eyes softening. He runs the back of his fingers over my cheek. "It's true. I've been too busy taking care of my family and trying to keep the streets of Silent Bend clean to form much of a relationship. And honestly, it's hard to bond with anyone with a normal life, when mine has been so…un-normal."

His eyes are soft and open. And I can see it there, that it's true.

"I'm sorry," I say, placing my hand over his and trapping his hand on my cheek. "I just—"

"It's okay," he interrupts. "But I take it that you're not a virgin, too."

I shrug, trying to be casual, but really, I'm ashamed. "Just once, the summer after high school. I'd just broken up with my high school boyfriend. You could say it was a rebound or revenge. Whatever it was, it was a mistake."

"That sounds super romantic," Ian says as he climbs off of me and back to the floor.

"Yeah, it was about as much as it sounds." He gives me a hand so I can slip to the edge of the counter. There's sugar caked on my entire back and everywhere in my hair. "You've got egg all over both of us."

"Now I'm delicious and smoking hot," he says with a wink. The timer goes off and I pull out some perfect cookies. I grab one and hand another to Ian. They're scalding hot, but I have baker's hands after all those years in the kitchen.

Ian takes a huge bite out of his cookie, no doubt burning his tongue. "Come on, let's go get cleaned up." He reaches out for me, and hand in hand, snacking on cookies made in the dark, we walk back toward the stairs.

We find Ian's and my clothes folded and placed on my bed. I blush at that. Did Rath really make those assumptions? But Ian takes his clothes and heads for one of the guest bathrooms while I shower in my own.

I pull on some cotton shorts and a tank when I get out and braid my hair over my shoulder. A minute later, Ian saunters back into my room and leans with his shoulder in the doorway.

"Well, I guess I'd better get back home," he says. He studies me, but it isn't demanding, or provocative. He's just seeing…me.

"You don't have to," I confess quietly. Because for the first time since moving here and living in this house, I haven't felt alone.

Neither of us says anything for a long time. We stare at each other, and there are a lot of thoughts going on. We know this can't end in a good way. He has his place in life and I have mine, whether I want it or not.

But we're here. And there's no question that we are something cosmic when we're together.

"Okay," he finally says quietly.

He flicks the light switch off. I turn off the light in the bathroom. We both climb into the gigantic bed, and I tuck myself into Ian's side. He presses a light kiss to my forehead, wrapping his arms around me.

Here. Here I am safe. Here I am understood.

And that's it.

We listen to each other breathe for a long while. And eventually, we sleep.

Fourteen

IAN ISN'T THERE WHEN I wake in the morning.

Somehow that doesn't surprise me. He's always doing stuff when he should be sleeping. I'm sure he had something to take care of. And he does have work today. He's doing a double shift.

So, with him out of the way, I spend the day planning my future. Because once again, I've just been waiting for the House to take control. It's time I take matters into my own hands.

At ten o'clock, after the sun has gone down, I walk down to the garage. There's a row of hooks that hold the keys. I grab the ones for the Jeep, because it's the least intimidating of all the vehicles.

The engine growls to life, and I carefully back out of the garage. With every day I spend here, I'm feeling more like things are mine. Like it's okay to touch and use them. I've been here for exactly a month now. I don't get lost in the house anymore. I know where things are. I've made a mess in my room, walked through the house naked. I'm feeling at home. This is the house my father lived in and where I should have grown up. The Conrath house feels like it was where I was supposed to end up all along.

The night is quiet and incredibly dark with the moon nothing more than a tiny sliver. I turn onto Main Street, drive a quarter of a mile, and take a left at the bakery. The road stretches on, through the swamp. And then there's the decaying, half-ruined House. I park right in front of the steps and climb out.

I knock on the front door three times and wait. I'm nervous, that's without question. But it's time I grow a backbone.

One of the Bitten I remember from my last visit opens the door. For a second, black veins surface on his face and his eyes brighten to a glowing yellow.

"I want to speak with Jasmine," I say, sounding confident, despite the immediate threat. I shove my way past him, pulling a stake from my purse.

He gives a small hiss when he sees it, but takes a step back. He's recognized me now, and I have no doubt he knows what it would mean if he kills me.

"Wait here," he says with disdain in his voice.

My palms are slick with sweat and my heart is racing. I slip the stake back into my purse. I stand there waiting, listening to the sounds of the House. Cameron and Trinity sound like they're playing a game somewhere. There's this metal singing sound I can't identify. And then there's a small scream somewhere upstairs, followed by a wet ripping sound.

Now I know where Markov is.

Movement to my right catches my eye.

The door to the library is cracked, and just inside I can see Christian. His fangs are deeply sunk into a woman's neck. Veins sprout out onto Christian's face, his eyes glowing. He takes one more pull and releases her. With control and careful movements, he lowers her to the ground.

The breath must catch in my throat because suddenly he looks up.

A smile crosses his face and he wipes a thumb at the blood under his lower lip and sucks it clean.

"Don't worry," he says as he walks out into the foyer. "She'll wake up in about an hour. The House had need for another Bitten."

"Oh," is all I manage.

He gives me another one of his smiles and starts up the stairs.

"Alivia." I look up as Jasmine rounds the corner. She has a pleasantly surprised smile on her face. "I wasn't expecting you this evening." But there's that annoyance hidden in her voice that says she didn't summon me, so why am I here?

"I know," I say, taking a quick, deep breath. I tell myself that I am technically a Born Royal and this is *my* House. I am ruler over her. "I wanted to discuss some terms with you."

"Terms," she repeats, a wary expression in her eyes.

Micah rounds the corner, and he stares me down coldly with his arms folded across his rather defined chest. And then comes Lillian, who doesn't look annoyed to see me.

"What kind of terms?" Jasmine continues.

"The terms of me claiming this House," I say.

All three of them grow silent and serious. Jasmine is thrown off, angry, surprised, maybe a little bit relieved. I've turned the tables on her, invading *her* life and imposing *my* wishes on her, and she doesn't know how to take my assertion.

"Let's talk," she finally responds. She extends her hand out toward the library.

I walk through the doors, and I'm shocked to see that everything looks back to normal. Maybe even better than it was before. The windows seem to have been replaced, covered once again. The bookshelves are repaired. There's no pool of blood on the floor. Only one stain on Jasmine's chair.

I'm tempted to sit in it, just to piss her off, but then I remember what she is, and I don't really want to die and resurrect tonight.

I choose to stand instead.

Jasmine sits in her chair. Micah sits beside her. Lillian sits on the couch and folds her hands elegantly over her lap.

"I know how badly you want the respect of the Royals again," I start. "If you claim me, you won't be shamed anymore. I can only imagine how hard it has been keeping the House afloat without any support." I play to Jasmine's sympathies. I need her to agree to my terms if I want to stay in control of my life. "But I also understand what may happen if the King comes."

I meet each of their eyes. Lillian seems understanding and nods as I speak. I decide I might like her. If I ever tried to gain an ally here in this House, she might be it. Micah just looks at me with disdain. We will never be on good terms.

"I will help you," I say, turning back to Jasmine, who watches me with impassive eyes. "I will claim the House, and I will help you get the respect you need back. By doing this, I know that the King will try and probably succeed in killing me. I'll resurrect and become a Born. But you have to wait a little while."

"How long?" Jasmine asks. "I've lead this shamed House for *fifteen* years."

"Just until January first," I say, letting it out in a breath. Because after that day, I'm surrendering my life as a human. "That's my twenty-third birthday. And if I'm going to stop aging, that seems a good one to be frozen at."

"What's wrong with being well seasoned?"

I turn to see Markov walk into the library. His face is covered in blood, it drips down onto his white, button up shirt. He dabs at himself with a handkerchief.

"Nothing," I squeak. "But I don't think you all want to wait until I'm an old woman."

"No," Jasmine says. "January first is just over three and a half months away. That's long enough."

"It gives us both time to prepare," I say. "You make whatever preparations you think will be helpful in protecting yourselves against the King. I get to say goodbye to being everything that makes me, me."

I look over at Lillian. She stares at the floor, and her eyes are haunted. I realize something then. Lillian resents being a vampire. She didn't ask for this. And I wonder if she got a nasty surprise when she woke up inside a grave. Not all Born can know what they are before they die.

"And what would you like in the meantime?" Jasmine asks with weight and hesitance in her voice.

I look back at her. "Nothing," I reply simply. "I will claim the House for you. We will say it's mine. But I don't want anything to do with it. My father didn't feel the need to be involved and neither do I. I won't forsake you, but I don't want your throne. And until my birthday, I just want to be left alone."

"That's fair," Lillian says. "You should take her up on her offer."

"You lack ambition, my child," Markov says. I look over at him. He's staring me down with that sly, scary smile of his. "You've been given the world on a silver platter, but you do not wish to partake."

"I agree to your terms," Jasmine quickly cuts him off. She doesn't want anyone planting any seedling ideas of power in my head. "The House will leave you be until January first. In exchange, you will claim the House and leave me to continue doing what I've been for the last fifteen years."

I step forward and extend a hand toward her. She stands, as well. Her eyes are cold and serious and she searches me. It's not hard to tell she's a woman who's been betrayed and stabbed in the back, and she's done the same to others. She's evaluating if I'm the same kind of person.

She takes my hand and shakes it.

When she releases it, I turn and head for the doorway. I pause though, turning back. "How are Trinity and Christian?"

"They're fine," Lillian says. She stands, as well, and crosses toward me. "It was a rough couple of hours, but they've both fully recovered."

"I'm glad to hear it. I've been worried about them." I look at Jasmine when I say this. And she's trying hard to cover the annoyance under her skin with a pleasant smile.

"Goodnight," I say, smiling back at her. Without another word, I turn and walk back out the front door.

Jasmine may be a tri-polar queen with an iron fist, but I won't be pushed around.

Fifteen

I'VE GOT THREE AND A half months until my life changes forever. Literally. I could sit here and wait for it. I could worry my time away over it. I could have sleepless nights as I think about saying goodbye to the sun, how blood is going to taste, how sharp my fangs will be.

Or I can keep living, right up to the very last second.

"You'll be here every mornin' at four?" Fred asks.

I nod. "I'm already used to the schedule," I say as we sit at the back of the bakery. The floor is covered in a fine dusting of flour. The air is heavy with the scent of dough. Fred, the large man with the darkest skin I've ever seen, has dried and cracked hands from the constant exposure to baking elements and endless washing. "So I promise it won't be a problem."

Fred, the owner and namesake of the bakery and coffee shop—*Fred's*—nods. "I need someone to help me Mondays, Wednesdays, and Thursdays. If that's good for you, I'll see you tomorrow morning."

A huge grin breaks over my face and I nod. "Thank you, sir. I appreciate the opportunity."

He just chuckles at me and shakes his head.

I show up the next morning at five minutes to four, bleary eyed, but ready to bake. Fred doesn't waste one second putting me to work.

And I'm happy to find that I've lost no skills in the last month that I haven't been working. When Fred sees that I can handle myself, he assigns me the scones, the cookies for the afternoon, and of course, the dishes.

At six-thirty, when the shop opens, a few people start trickling in. Getting their breakfast on their way to work. Grabbing coffee, brewed by the self-proclaimed master, Tina. Fred helps the customers while I work in the back.

At ten, I'm just bringing out the sheet of snickerdoodle cookies when I hear my name called from the door. I look up to see Sheriff McCoy walking in.

"Are you workin' here?" he asks with a look between a scowl and confusion.

"Yeah," I say as I slide the cookies onto the display rack.

"Why?" he asks in bewilderment.

"Because why not?" I resist spitting the words out. Barely.

More customers wander into the shop. I'm surprised at how busy it is in here, considering how small the town is. I haven't been up front until now, but I've been hearing the foot traffic all day.

"Fred, who's this lovely young woman helping you out today?" a man in construction garb asks with a flirtatious smile as he walks up to the counter. He's followed by a whole crew who starts ordering coffee.

"This is, uh…" Fred says as he takes money from a customer and checks them out. "Alivia Ryan. She's new in town. And one hell of a baker."

"New in town," the man says with an approving smile. "Don't get too many of them types here."

Luke gives the guy a disapproving look. "Leave her alone, Dallas."

"What?" Dallas says, with an innocent expression. "I was just bein' friendly."

"You look familiar," one of Dallas' buddies says as he squints in my direction, coffee cup in hand. "You related to someone here in town?"

My eyes dart uncomfortably from the guy to Luke. Who just gives me a little *I told you so* look back.

"Wait a second," the guy says, still studying my face. "You're that girl who moved into the Conrath Estate, huh? You're that freak's daughter."

"Now, Corbin," Fred says, fixing the guy with a cold stare, even as my stomach settles somewhere in the vicinity of my feet. "You's a grown man now and should know words like that isn't nice. I think you ought to apologize to this nice young woman."

But I've been outed. And there are two other people in the shop looking at me now like I'm about to tear into their necks at any second.

"I'm sorry," I respond snarkily. "Did you think you know who I am?"

Dallas gives an "oh!"—fist to the mouth and everything. I offer Corbin a peeved off smile as I walk back into the kitchen.

And it's like that for the next week. People talk about me in low voice like I can't hear them. They speculate. There's constant talk about the House. About the year 1875. About blood and missing or dead loved ones.

But never once do I hear the actual word vampire.

My shift is from four to eleven. It's not many hours or days, but I don't need the money. Not at all. I need the normalcy. But this is hardly normal. When everyone looks at you with disdain or fear. When you're constantly judged for the sins of your father.

I've just finished putting the cinnamon rolls in the display case at six-fifteen when the little bell above the door rings. I look up, dusting my hands off on my apron. In walks a woman, maybe in her upper forties. She's rail thin, almost skeletal. Her cheekbones are sharp and prominent, her lips too full for her face. But it's instantly her eyes that draw me.

She wears sunglasses, but behind them, I can see hollow eye sockets. Her blindness explains the walking stick.

"Good morning," I say to her politely. "You're up and about early."

"I'm afraid I don't get much sleep these days," she says with a pleasant smile. "I've been up too long already this morning."

She bumps into a table, nearly knocking a chair over. I duck around the counter and help guide her to the display case. "Sorry about that," she laughs at herself. "I'm a lot clumsier than I used to be."

"It's okay," I reassure her. "We're not quite open yet, but we've got some stuff out. What can I get you? I just brought out the cinnamon rolls. We've got raspberry scones, bran muffins, fritters. Just about any breakfast pastry, we've got it."

"Mmm," she says in delight. Her accent is heavily Southern Belle. "It all smells heavenly. How about a cinnamon roll?"

"Excellent choice," I say as I scoop one out for her onto a little glass plate. "That'll be two dollars."

The woman digs around in her bag and pulls out a wallet. When she opens it, I see different bills folded in different ways. Smart. She hands me a five and I make change for her.

"Thank you, my dear," she says as I take her plate to one of the tables and guide her to it. "I just moved in to the edge of town and hoped I might find somewhere comparable to my old regular. Y'all are very sweet here."

"I haven't been in Silent Bend too long myself," I say, sitting at the table for a minute because I don't have much else to do in the back at the moment.

"That right?" she says with a smile and manages to fork some of the roll off.

"I've only been here at Fred's for a week," I say. It's nice, having a normal conversation.

"How do you like the town so far?" she asks.

"It's…" How the hell do I answer that question? Dark. Manipulated. Totally crazy. "It's a town that will keep you on your toes."

"Good to know," she says.

"Well, I better get back to work," I say, standing from the table. "You have a nice day."

"You too, Miss…?" she asks.

"Alivia, Alivia Ryan."

"Well, it's nice to meet you. I'm Daphne, and I'm sure you'll be seeing a lot more of me."

"I hope so," I respond politely. Fred calls for me from the back, and I go to help him.

Flour. Sugar. Eggs. Chocolate. Berries.

All of this is normal. And when I have my headphones in, listening to my old playlist, it's like I'm back in Colorado and life is what it used to be.

Until just after eight, Fred comes in the back where I'm putting the peanut butter chocolate chip cookies in the oven. "Ian Ward is at the counter askin' for you. You two even know each other?"

I blush, even though Fred has no idea of the truth. Boy, do we… "Yeah," I say instead, tucking my hair behind my ear. Fred takes over, and I walk out to the counter.

There are two ladies drinking coffee in one corner and enjoying scones. And standing at the counter, hands in the pockets of his EMT uniform, easy as always, is Ian.

"I have to admit, I didn't really believe Rath when he told me you'd gotten a job at Fred's," he says with the classic Ian smile. "This seems too mundane and normal for you."

"Well, this girl doesn't have bills to pay like some people," I say, recalling the conversation we had that first day we met. "But I needed something to keep me busy and from going crazy."

Ian just nods with a smile and studies me for a moment. "You look good."

And he means it. Which is a surprise, since I'm wearing a maroon apron covered in flour, my hair is in a crazy, messy bun on top of my head, and I probably have foodstuff on my face somewhere.

"Thanks," I say with a blush. "You just get off work?"

Ian nods and I instantly notice the tiredness in his eyes. "Yep, should be my only graveyard shift this week, though. Worked the last six days straight. I'm going home now to catch a few hours of sleep, but…maybe I can come by later this evening?"

He looks hopeful, like he isn't sure what my answer is going to be. Which is incredibly adorable. And I'd almost never use that word in relation to Ian. Strong? Yes. Assertive? Yes. Adorable…?

"Yeah," I answer with a smile as another customer walks through the door. "I think you can."

He just laughs and his eyes grow brighter. "Well, how about three scones for the family while I'm here? Lula loves Fred's heart-stopping pastries."

"You got it."

Sixteen

"DON'T TAKE OFFENSE BECAUSE I genuinely want to know," I say to Rath as we eat dinner on the veranda. The cook has outdone herself today, and the girl who serves us won't look me in the eye, as usual. "But what do you do all day?"

Rath looks up at me, and I can't read his eyes because he's wearing sunglasses, which only makes me wonder about his species all the more. "I manage the affairs of the Estate."

"Yes, I know," I say in exasperation. "But what does that mean?"

Rath sets his wine glass back on the table. I've notice that he drinks one glass with dinner every night. Never more, never less. "I manage the crew that takes care of the grounds. I order supplies. I handle the financials involved with the Estate. That occupies most of my time."

I take a sip of my sweet tea, something I'm coming to like. "Henry should have left the Estate to you, not me. You deserve it. It's easy to see you love this place."

"I do love it," Rath says as he leans back in his chair and overlooks the grounds. "But my devotion has always been to the

Conrath family. I don't need money or the esteem. I am here for you, Alivia."

I observe Rath for a moment. His expression is sad, regretful. "You miss Henry, don't you?"

Rath doesn't look back at me when he says, "I do."

"You more than just worked for my father," I say as I pick up a roll and pick at it. It's dry. Mine are better. "You two were best friends."

Rath sits back up and begins cutting his steak again. "Bonds run deep when loyalty is proven in both directions over and over again. When you've been through trials of fire and still stand by one another's side. Your father was my brother."

It's hard for me to imagine such loyalty and love. And not the romantic kind of love because I don't think that's what this is for one second. Which is what makes it so strange. I never knew Henry, never saw him with Rath. But I can see what Henry's death has done to Rath, it's there in his face, in his very countenance, every day.

"Thank you for being here for me," I say, reaching out across the table and resting my hand on Rath's wrist. "I know we don't know each other well, but it's comforting to have you here. Like...there's still a small part of my father that's lived on through you. It's far better than having nothing. And thank you for your loyalty. That isn't lost on me."

Rath looks up at me and with his free hand, removes his sunglasses. His eyes are so dark that I can't tell iris from pupil. "You are always welcome. And my loyalty will always lie with your family, even after you resurrect."

In three and a half months. I should tell him that. But somehow it feels like a defeat.

We finish our meal in silence, but it's comfortable. A new bond has formed between us. Not many words were spoken, but the meaning runs deep.

Just as Angelica has come to clear our plates, there's a knock on the glass window behind me. I turn to see Ian's eyes searching the property behind us.

"Excuse me," I say to Rath, who simply goes stony-faced and nods.

I walk back into the ballroom and find myself looking over my shoulders, checking for Bitten spying on us from the shadows of the trees.

"I parked off the main road and walked in," Ian says quietly for some reason. "Why is your driveway so damn long?"

I laugh and slip my fingers through Ian's. "Don't blame me, that was all Henry."

Without thinking about it, I lead us upstairs because the staff is still going about their duties on the main floor. They all usually wrap up around seven, and it's just past six-thirty.

We slip into my bedroom and close the door behind us. And the second it is, Ian wraps his hands around my waist and brings my lips to his.

"I've missed you," he growls into my mouth.

"It's only been a week and a half," I tease him. He backs us into a wall and that sends an explosion of sparks shooting through my body. My hands snake under his shirt, tracing over his muscular back.

"A veritable eternity," he breathes as he lets me slip his shirt off over his head.

"You shouldn't go getting ideas in your head about this," I say as our lips reconnect. "I just really need some of...this." I run my hands up over his abs, over his very defined chest muscles.

"It's all yours," he says with a smile against my lips.

Ian hoists me up and I wrap my legs around his waist. Like I weigh nothing at all, he turns and crosses the room to the bed. He topples us onto it.

"It really has been a long ten days," Ian says as he runs a hand along my cheek and looks down at me. "I couldn't get away from work and Lula was in a bad way for a few days."

"It's okay," I say, absentmindedly tracing a finger up and down the valley between his abs. "I've been busy, too."

"I can't believe you went and got a job at Fred's," he says with a chuckle.

I smile back, because working in the bakery is the most natural thing in the world for me, but then I also come home to *this* house every afternoon. "Well, I've not just been busy with work. I went to see Jasmine last week."

Ian's face turns a shade whiter and his expression falls. "What?"

I swallow hard. I'm an adult, I don't have to justify anything. This is my decision. But I do know how Ian feels about me mingling with the House members.

"I wasn't just going to wait around again for the House to decide what to do with me," I start. Ian rolls onto his side and we lie there facing each other. "I made a deal with her."

"A deal with the House is never good," he says, barely suppressing a hiss.

"Hear me out, please," I ask softly.

Ian looks away from me for a moment. His jaw is tight and he looks a bit like he wants to hit something. There's rage and fight and darkness in Ian. So much of it. But most of the times he looks at me, I see something different. Something softer.

With great effort, he takes a second, calms himself down, and looks back at me. "Okay."

I tell him everything. How I agreed to claim the House, but not until after my birthday. How I didn't let Jasmine manipulate me into anything. How I thought Lillian might be an ally if I needed one. How Markov brought everything I was giving up to my attention.

"It's damn scary that you walked right back into that House," Ian says. His eyes are open, receptive—not angry. "But it sounds like you know what you're doing. Maybe like you're even supposed to be doing this. I'm glad you're not getting involved, but I think you would have been a great House leader. And that, coming from me, says something."

And this just brings to light everything that's doomed about our relationship. That hurts, so much because every time I look at Ian, I see everything that makes me okay with this new life. I see hope and excitement. Acceptance.

"We have three and a half months," I say quietly. "That's all I could get us. But it's ours. They promised to leave me alone."

Ian rolls forward and kisses my lips and everything in me craves more. Which just brings fear into my heart. "You just have to promise me one thing," I say as I push him away an inch or two.

"What?" he asks, unsure eyes searching mine.

"You have to promise not to fall in love with me." And when I say it, I'm gravely serious.

Because it's my greatest fear right now. More than being killed by a demented king. More than knowing I will resurrect. More than a future of craving blood. My greatest fear is what I'm feeling now and how much more of it I'll be feeling the longer this goes on. And then to have that ripped away…

Ian doesn't answer me right away. He studies me, and I know the self-reflection that's going on in his head. It's the same story for me. "That's going to be a hard promise to keep, I'm afraid."

"But you have to make it," I say, feeling desperate. I place my hands on his chest, but my eyes fall away from his. I can't look at him. "Because we have an expiration. And this will have to end."

Ian's breathing grows slightly faster and deeper. Heat rises in his eyes. He's angry about this and this situation that I didn't ask for— the one that neither of us can do anything about.

"Three and a half months," he says with hardness in his voice. "Those three and a half months are ours, and if any of them mess with a single day of it, I'll kill them all."

Seventeen

"I KNOW THAT YOU'RE PERFECTLY capable of cooking Thanksgiving dinner, Lula," I say in exasperation. "But I just thought it would be nice if I helped you with a few things. I work in a bakery, I could do the rolls and it really would be no problem."

"Girl, you get outa' my house and stop tryin' to impose on ma' family," Lula growls at me. She literally shakes a frying pan at me.

I turn to Ian, exasperation on my face. "A little help here?"

"I...psh," he says with a shrug and a shake of his head.

"Really?" I say, completely and utterly annoyed. "Look, Lula—"

"I said get outta' my house!" she bellows at me.

I raise my hands in surrender and walk out the back door.

"Liv, wait!" Ian calls as he follows me out into the backyard.

"Wait for what?" I yell as he jogs and stops in front of me. "Your grandmother hates me. She won't even let me in the door most days. Thanksgiving is in two days and she keeps saying she has all week to buy the food. There's going to be nothing left at the market!"

"Yes, I know she's completely bat-shit crazy," Ian says as he puts his hands on my upper arms. "And she sleeps through half the day

148

most days and Thanksgiving won't be any different. Let's you and I go right now and get the food. She won't know any different."

I take a deep breath, trying to calm myself down. "Why is your grandmother such a bitch to me?"

"Did you just call my ancient, wrinkly, half-crazy grandmother a bitch?" Ian laughs.

"Well, that's what she is!"

Ian shakes his head with another laugh. "Yeah, she is." He takes my hand and starts walking me to his van. "But honestly, I think she hates you because she knows what you're going to be someday."

"You told her?!" I gasp in horror.

"No, no!" he reassures me as he opens the passenger door for me. I slip in and Ian rests in the doorframe. "Lula has just always had this…vampdar."

"A vampdar?" I ask in bored disbelief.

"A vampire radar," Ian just says as a smile tugs on one side of his mouth. "She just knows when one is close by, other than that one time she slept through one breaking into her house. But she knows. Even if you aren't a vampire yet."

"Hm," I say, crossing my arms over my chest. "Key word is *yet*."

"Let it go," he says as he leans in and presses a kiss to my lips. I try to glare at him as he backs up and walks around the van to the driver's seat.

Over the past month and a half, Ian and I have become experts in going out into town together without appearing to be together. Because with him being an enemy of the House and me having claim over it and all, it won't lead to any good, us being seen together by anyone.

So we go to stores together. We each take our own baskets, grab our own food. We pass by each other in the aisles, only slyly making eye contact. We checkout separately and one of us returns to the car and the other follows a few minutes later. That's the dangerous part, when we drive together. Most days we don't risk it.

We've gone to restaurants together, but separate. I manage to drag out Rath every so often—it's pretty rare. Ian brings along Elle. We catch each other's eyes. Smile knowingly and continue with our separate meals.

And most nights one of us sneaks to the other's house.

It's a weird, disjointed relationship. We both know our expiration date is approaching, but it doesn't make it any less delicious before that day.

"ALIVIA, WAKE UP."

My eyes squint open to find Ian lying right in front of me, his nose only an inch from mine. A smile is already splitting his face. The little wrinkles he gets around his mouth and eyes when he does so sends a wave of happiness through my soul.

"I've got a surprise for you."

"What is it?" I ask, sleepily rubbing an eye.

"Don't ask questions, just get dressed."

So I do. It's cold, even in the house, the last Sunday in November. I pull on a sweater and jeans. Barely able to contain his excitement, Ian takes my hand the second I'm done and drags me down the stairs and out the door. We pile into his van, and he heads down the driveway.

"Ian, where are we going?" I ask with a laugh. His excitement is contagious.

"I realized that in this town, I'm never going to be able to take you on a proper date," he says as he takes one of my hands in his. He raises it to his lips and presses a kiss to the back of my hand. "So I thought we'd get out of town for the day. I wanted to go overnight, but I know you have to work tomorrow morning."

"You're making me think I should call Fred and tell him I'm sick," I say as I raise an eyebrow at Ian.

"I'm thinking maybe you should," he responds, a hungry look in his eyes.

We drive two hours north to Jackson. I flew into the city when I arrived, but immediately left it. It's a city, much like any other. A mix of old and new buildings. Rolling greenery.

Ian pulls his van into a parking spot outside a restaurant and takes me inside. It smells like potatoes and eggs and bacon and every other amazing breakfast food.

"Table for two?" the hostess says. Ian nods and she takes us to a table toward the back, right next to a window.

After we order, Ian takes both of my hands in his, pressing my knuckles to his lips. He stares at me, studying me in the deepest sense of the word.

"What?" I say with a happy smile. "Why are you looking at me like that?"

A small smile pulls at his lips and he shakes his head. "I just... I just wish that we could do this, all the time. Without hiding and being on our toes every second of the day."

My eyes soften and his words melt all the female parts inside of me. "I know."

And I imagine it for a moment. The two of us running away, leaving Mississippi. Going to...Nebraska. Surely there aren't any vampires in Nebraska. We could live a normal life without kissing in the shadows or behind closed doors. We could just be...together.

But I can't say any of those things. Because I made Ian make me a promise, and I have to keep it, too. And I will only do that by not daydreaming too hard.

"What do you want to do today?" he asks as the waitress brings us our brunch. "What could we never do in Silent Bend?"

"Um," I take a moment to mull it over as I take a bite of the French toast. "All of those cliché first date things normal people get to do. A movie. A walk in the park. Ice cream."

"It's only like forty-five degrees outside, Liv," Ian chuckles as he bites into a piece of toast. "You want ice cream?"

"I want ice cream," I laugh at myself and him. I pucker out my lower lip in a pout for effect.

"Alright," he says. "The woman wants ice cream, so she'll get ice cream."

I want to say that I only want to go out for ice cream with him, but that's just too much for our very few weeks we have left. So instead, I simply lean over the table, and Ian meets me halfway. Slowly, softly, our lips linger.

As people walk by on the street outside that window right next to us. Here we are, kissing, being together, for everyone in Jackson to see. And for this moment, I don't care who sees.

"I'M REALLY SORRY TO LEAVE you hanging last minute," I say into my cell phone that night. I cough for effect. "I just don't want to bring the plague into the shop."

"Don' worry about nothin,'" Fred says on the other end. "I'll get things takin' care of. You rest up."

"Thanks, Fred," I say. I feel bad for lying to him since he's being so kind and understanding. "I'm sure I'll be fine by Wednesday."

We say our goodbyes and I hang up.

The city of Jackson is laid out before me. Our hotel room is on the seventh floor, which isn't very high, but it isn't the most vertical city. City lights twinkle in the dark and it's just beautiful. Made all the more beautiful by the perfect beautiful day I've just had.

Ian and I did all those mundane, normal date things. We saw a chick-flick, took a walk through the freezing cold park after we got our ice cream. We held hands and kissed and cuddled for all to see.

I'm going to miss all of this when we have to leave in the morning.

A sliver of light cuts through the dark hotel room. I turn to see Ian walking out of the bathroom, a burst of steam following him from the shower he's just taken.

He wears a pair of sweats I've seen him sleep in many times. But his chest is bare. And I bare no shame as I let my eyes wander over his skin.

Cut chest. Rising and falling valley of stomach muscles. Shoulders that beg me to touch them. Scars dot his body here and there, but they only add to the rugged beauty that is this man who I wish could be mine. Forever.

Ian's eyes never once leave mine as he slowly crosses the room to me. And with every step he takes, I feel my temperature rising a few degrees.

Finally, an eternity later, he stops just an inch from me. "You're so beautiful, Alivia." His fingers hesitantly come to my sides, sending sparks racing through my body. His nose brushes mine, his lips just a breath away.

He smells like soap and heat and desire, and it leaves my head spinning. His still wet hair drips onto his shoulders, and my own wet hair drips down my back, soaking the oversized shirt I'm wearing over my underwear.

"I don't want to leave tomorrow," he whispers. He traces his nose over my cheek, and then his lips are brushing against my ear.

"Just pretend tonight is all there is," I breathe. "It's just us. Just tonight."

His lips kiss my ear, and then they part and his teeth send an explosion of desire rocketing through my veins.

Suddenly, the inch of space between us is far too much and I am not in possession of my own body when I clasp my hands behind his neck and wrap both of my legs firmly around his waist.

It's just Ian. Just me.

Eighteen

A FEW DAYS LATER, I'VE just woken up when there's a quiet knock on my door. I squint my eyes open just as Ian lets himself in. A smile starts to spread on my lips. This is a habit he's formed, one I greatly approve of. Without hesitation, Ian climbs into my bed and wraps his arms around me.

"Good morning," I say sleepily. I press my face into his chest. And then my nose crinkles. "You just got off work, didn't you? You smell like ambulance and blood."

"I did." And the tone of his voice instantly brings my eyes up to his face.

"What happened?" I ask. Because I've been in this town long enough to know that something did happen.

Ian sighs and holds me tighter. I place my head back on his chest. "There was a thirteen-year-old girl attacked the day we left for Jackson, on the edge of town. Her mom found her outside their house the next morning. She was almost completely drained of blood."

"Almost?" I question.

"Yeah," he says. He rubs his eyes. He's tired, he needs sleep. But lately he comes here first after a shift. Sometimes he then goes home and sleeps, sometimes he just sleeps here. "And then there was another attack last night. You know Bella who volunteers at the library?"

"I've only met her once, but yeah," I say, recalling the very unfriendly redheaded woman. The one who looked at me differently the second I asked for any info on the Conrath Plantation.

My insides are sinking.

"She was nearly drained, too. She was found at her house by the neighbor."

"They were both *nearly* drained," I say. The room grows colder and my future comes creeping up on me. "Too much blood gone for it to have been a House member feeding, too much blood gone for them to survive and be turned into a Bitten." And that means just dead.

Ian rubs a hand up and down my arm absentmindedly. "I think someone was trying to turn them, they just didn't have enough self-control. If it was just a thirsty vamp, they wouldn't have left just a little blood. They always drain them. I think these two were a mistake—a mess up."

"Whoever declared war on the House is back," I say as I sit up and look down at Ian. "That's how it started before. Someone went missing, and then they attacked the House."

Ian nods, his eyes distant. "I don't know what to do about this," he says. "I can't stop it if I don't know who's doing this. I've been patrolling at nights, but I've never seen anyone. I want to blame the House, but it's clearly not them. People are scared, Liv. Half this town is fully aware of the vampire problem in Silent Bend. They never talk about it, but they're going to start."

And I can only imagine the chaos that is going to happen if the town goes into a vampire panic.

"I should go talk to Jasmine," I say. "See if they've heard anything. I'm sure they've been on alert. They might have some leads."

"No," Ian shakes his head and his eyes grow dark with worry. His hand reaches forward and his thumb rests on my lower lip. "You're only a month away from your birthday. You show up at their door now with all this chaos going on, Jasmine might decide she's tired of waiting. It's too risky, Liv."

"You're not my protector," I say with annoyance as I stand and take a step away from the bed.

"But he's right." Rath pushes the door open and stands in the doorway with his hands folded. "Jasmine is a desperate, oftentimes unpredictable leader. If you go to her, anything could happen."

I look between Ian and Rath, angry and conflicted.

I'm not a little girl. I've survived on my own the last four years without anyone's help. Without a father figure or an overly protective non-boyfriend.

But something is tugging on the back of my heart. Something soft and grateful that there are two men in my life who care about me and that I'm not alone.

It's annoying. So I walk into the bathroom and close the door on them.

"WHAT'S BOTHERING YOU, ALIVIA?"

I look up from the display case to Daphne. She sits at a table, eating her cinnamon roll. It's early, just after six again. She's the first customer of the morning. Not every day, but I usually see her twice a week.

"How do you know something is wrong?" I ask as I slide the scones onto the display tray.

"I don't need eyes to feel the frustration rolling off of you," she says. "You've been quiet today. What's on your mind?"

I sigh and walk around the display case and lean against it. I cross my arms over my chest. "Life is just complicated," I say, because I could never explain what's really bothering me. Four weeks, one day. A non-boyfriend who's agitated and I'm afraid is going to do something stupid. Rath insisting I not go to the House. "I never thought I'd be involved in politics. All of adult life is just a game of politics, I'm learning."

"Sadly, it's true," Daphne says with the nod of her head. "And it's even more true when you live in a small, old town like this one."

"Yeah," I say. I stand back up and grab the baking sheet.

"You come grab these biscuits?" Fred calls from the back.

"Coming."

AND ALL THAT WEEK, PEOPLE talk about the attacks. The fear and the speculation builds and builds.

At some point, it's all going to explode.

ON DECEMBER NINTH, CORBIN, THE man who got all worked up at Fred's the second he found out I was of Conrath blood, shoots an innocent man who is out too late one night, because Corbin was convinced he was a vampire.

On December tenth, Sheriff McCoy arrests another woman for breaking into her best friend's house, sure she was feeding off of her husband at nights.

December eleventh, Rath shows me another secret door in my bedroom that opens into an armory. There's nothing else to call it. The small room is stocked with guns, crossbows, stakes, knives—anything and everything deadly.

I have to be ready to protect myself with the town so on edge.

December twelfth is the day I finally realize that I haven't seen Ian in two days. Which is out of character and scary. We're down to nineteen days, and Ian wouldn't waste any of them.

Something's wrong.

"Damn it," I hiss at my phone when Ian doesn't answer. He hasn't responded to any of my texts, either.

Shoving my cell phone into the back pocket of my jeans, I grab the keys to the Jeep from the hook and open the garage. Just as I'm about to open the driver's door, a car rolls up behind it.

Elle climbs out of the rust bucket and I remember that she's just turned sixteen.

"Have you seen Ian?" she asks with worry in her voice.

"I've been trying to get ahold of him all day. I haven't seen him since Wednesday." Fear and anticipation leap into my chest and threaten to choke me.

"He came home from work this morning in a *really* bad mood," Elle says. She clutches the hem of her shirt and twists the fabric absentmindedly. "I went to the cabin to try and talk to him about what was wrong. I didn't even go to my first two classes this morning 'cause I was worried about him. But he wouldn't tell me anything. He just kept talking to himself and looking at the maps of town. He was twirling a stake the whole time."

"Something happened at work last night," I say as I watch the sun sink behind the house. "I don't know if he's told you how there's been two attacks in the last week. There had to be another one."

"He told me," she says in that gentle voice of hers. I've never noticed the necklace Elle wears until now. It's a long silver cord and on the end of it is a simple narrow shaft. And suddenly, I have no doubt it's really a needle with the toxin inside of it. "But he said he didn't know how to fix it."

I swear under my breath. "I think I know where he's planning to go. You're blocking me in, so you drive."

Elle doesn't ask questions as I direct her. She stares straight out the window, fingers gripped white-knuckled on the steering wheel. Her jaw is clenched tightly. But she's calm and quiet. It's kind of disturbing how collected she always is.

"Park here," I say as we get within a mile. "Pull into the trees so no one can see the car. We'll walk in from here."

The underbrush is thick, and the ground is wet and smelly. It's half swamp from here to the House.

"I wanted to talk to the House about the attacks," I explain as we carefully work our way through the brush and muck. "Ian was too scared to let me go, but they're the only ones who might know something. And Ian knows that."

"But they hate my brother," Elle says, fear showing in her voice.

I nod.

It was bad when I walked into the House the first time. They could have killed me right then. But I would have resurrected.

Ian won't resurrect. If they kill him, he'll die. And while the House had no hard feelings toward me other than the choices of my father, they have every reason to hate Ian.

I start walking faster.

The House comes into view, and my heart breaks into a sprint when I see Ian's van parked right in front.

"What's the plan?" Elle whispers as we get closer. "They can't know you two are together. I only brought three doses and my blowgun. We can't take them all down to get him out of there."

I don't really have a plan. I didn't think. I have nothing. No stakes, no crossbow, nothing. I just rushed out. Pure protective instinct.

"Let's just get close and see if we can hear or see anything," I whisper.

We creep up onto the back veranda. It's going to be difficult to see anything since they've covered all the windows. But this house is falling apart.

We find a board that had been nailed over a hole and is now peeling away.

I can just see into the foyer through the great room.

There's Jasmine, Markov, Anna, and Micah. Ian stands before them. With a crossbow hanging in one hand. To the untrained eye, it would look relaxed, unready. But I see the muscles in his arm strained, his finger hovering near the trigger.

"You do realize who that woman is, right?" Ian says. There's annoyance heavy in his voice. He extends a hand out back toward town. "She is Mayor Jackson's wife. People are going to start asking questions and you're who they are all going to turn on. Do you not remember what happened to Elijah Conrath? To half of his House members?"

"You've got a lot of nerve coming here," Micah hisses. "Acting like we've been sitting on our asses, doing nothing about this."

"It sure doesn't seem like you have," Ian accuses.

Markov hisses. He's angled toward me, and even from here, I see his fangs extend.

I'm about to spring from our hiding spot and start pounding on the doors when Cameron wanders by. He's holding a bowl of chips. "Y'all just need to chill out. Here," he extends his snack out to them all. "Maybe everyone's just hangry. You want some?"

"Cameron, get the hell out of here," Anna hisses with annoyance. "And quit trying to get high. It obviously doesn't work anymore."

"The worst tragedy in the world," he mutters regretfully as he shuffles to the stairs.

"Jaz," Micah growls. "Why don't you just let me kill him now? You're just letting him stand there, armed, in your house."

"Down, boy," Jasmine says coldly and with the hint of annoyance in her voice.

"I just don't understand how you could have nine of you here and not know anything," Ian continues. "You all got *attacked*, and you've found nothing."

"Looks like you're slacking on your job, vamp slayer," Micah growls back.

"Well, like I said, there's only one of me and nine of you," Ian says in a low voice as he takes a step toward him. His grip on the crossbow tightens.

"Enough," Jasmine says. I just about lose it when she places her hand on Ian's chest and shoves him away from Micah. "I will admit, we've not been paying enough attention to this problem. We've had other issues to handle."

The preparations for when King Cyrus comes and they hand me over to him. The fall in Ian's expression tells me he knows exactly what she's talking about.

"But we will make more of an effort. Micah, I want you and the Kask brothers out every night looking for this intruder." She looks back at her lover.

Who doesn't look pleased. But he nods.

"Fine," Ian says as he turns for the door. "About time you put that hot head man-whore to use."

And I would have let loose the scream if Elle hadn't clasped her hand around my mouth.

Ian is standing in the doorway when Micah jumps on him. Fangs extended, muscled body rippling and flying through the air. They collide and go tumbling down the stairs.

But Micah howls in pain, covering his eyes. It's still six and the sun is not yet sunk into the horizon. His eyes are burning in pain. Micah scrambles back into the house.

Ian clambers along the ground away from the House, still barely grasping the crossbow. There's a hint of fear in his eyes, but even more, there's lividity. "Touch me again and I swear I'll stake you!"

"I see you again and you're dead!" Micah roars. But his pride is wounded. He stalks back into the House without another word or a backward glance.

"I suggest you never come back." Jasmine is stone cold. She shuts the door in Ian's face, and my view of him is cut off.

"We should go," Elle whispers. "We should go now."

I'm shaking and trembling. I can hear Micah upstairs throwing a tantrum. Crashing sounds, hissing roars of frustration. Jasmine speaks quietly to Markov, but I can't hear anything anymore.

"Let's go." Elle grabs my wrist and starts leading me off the veranda. I stumble along after her numbly. Through the trees and the swamp, back toward her car.

Ian just went and ruined everything.

Nineteen

THE ENTIRE DRIVE HOME, ELLE tries to call Ian. He doesn't answer her calls. He doesn't answer mine. So we head straight back to the Ward property.

And we both sigh a big breath of relief when we find Ian's van parked next to the cabin. We pile out of the car and barge through the front door.

Ian looks up at us from a duffle bag he's packing. For a moment, he seems surprised to see us together. But then his eyes are cold and hard.

"What the hell were you thinking?" I blurt. I take five aggressive steps to close the distance between us and shove him in the chest. Hard.

He stumbles back two steps and clenches his teeth, his lips pursed. His fingers ball into fists, his nostrils flare as he lets out a hard breath. For a second, I think he's going to hit me.

"We saw you tonight. Your sister, who *you're* supposed to be protecting," I poke him in the chest, "and I, we, followed you to the House tonight. We saw you acting like an idiot. We saw Micah attack you." My voice cracks. Suddenly, tears have welled up in my eyes and my throat feels tight. And that makes me angry.

I don't want to care this much.

I don't want to be this scared for someone else.

"You can't do stuff like that, Ian," Elle says quietly. I look over at her. There are no tears in her eyes, but she's pale and scared. "They hate you already. Don't give them a reason to kill you."

"I can't just sit by and do nothing," Ian hisses. His fingers flex and clench harder. "You know who got attacked last night? The mayor's wife. That's right, Dotty Jackson was attacked. Her husband called 911 because she was lying there like she was in a coma. And just as we got there, she woke up, bit her husband, and took off. I couldn't catch her. And now she's out there in Silent Bend, rabid and wild and out of control, with a Debt to a faceless enemy. Someone is trying to take our town down. And I'm not going to just sit by and let this happen. If the House isn't going to do anything about it, then I will."

He opens a cupboard, grabs a shotgun, and throws it into his bag.

"But you can't go running around pissing Jasmine and the House off," I say, my fire dimming, being smothered out by my fear. "Especially Micah. He will do anything for Jasmine. And Markov is just plain psychotic. He'll kill you for fun and do it with a smile on his face."

"Ian, please listen to her," Elle whispers.

He stalks across the room and pulls the cushions off the couch to retrieve a huge handful of stakes.

"I'm going to find this terrorist, and I'm going to stop them." Ian zips up the bag and slings it over his shoulder. He shoves his way between Elle and I and opens the door.

"Ian, please." I grab his wrist and make him stop.

He hesitates. His eyes shift to me, and for just a moment, they soften. For just a second, I think I've convinced him to stay. To not go run out into the night with a death wish.

He leans down, presses a soft, lingering kiss to my lips. And then he walks out the door.

"Ian!" I yell frantically. But he doesn't turn back.

Elle and I watch him back down the driveway. He doesn't look at either of us.

"You know there's no stopping him, right?" Elle says softly. She reaches out and takes my hand.

"I know." Because I do.

ELLE DRIVES ME HOME, AND it's nearly eleven by the time I walk through the front doors. I would have asked her to stay with me tonight, to try and protect her. But she has Lula, and since Ian is out trying to get himself killed, it's now up to Elle to protect her. And there's no way I could have convinced Lula to come to my house.

I don't know what to do. I want to ask Rath for help, but once Ian sets his mind to something, there's no stopping him. Rath couldn't force Ian to go into hiding. That's just not Ian.

I want to go to Jasmine, beg for her not to hurt Ian. To tell Micah to let it go. But I can't do that. I can't protect Ian. I can't protect this town.

To combat the feeling of helplessness, I sit on the front porch with a crossbow. I've got a box full of arrows. And a glass of sweet tea on the other side of me. It's freezing out here. My toes are numb and my fingers are stiff.

Knowing what Ian is out doing, the night feels dark and dense. It feels like it hides things. Demons lurk in the shadows, stare at me with hidden eyes. It's a night that feels like anything terrible and horrifying could happen.

One o'clock.

Two o'clock.

Three o'clock.

My eyes grow heavy. But I do not sleep.

Around four-thirty, it happens.

There's a sound. It's an unidentifiable one, but I know it's there and there hasn't been any other sounds all night.

I stand on the porch, straining my eyes in the dark. But I'm not a vampire yet and I can't see much of anything. My movement, however, turns on the motion sensor light, flooding everything within fifty feet of the house in light.

A gargled scream cuts through the silent night and a *thwack* falls on my ears. Red eyes flash for a brief second. The sound of scattering gravel and a scuffle sound out.

"Who's there?" I yell, bringing my crossbow up to eyelevel. I dart off of the porch and ten feet out. "I'm armed and if you don't like the feel of wood splinters in your heart, you should get off of my property!"

Fangs flash, and as something hits the ground, another figure leaps out at me with the glint of yellow eyes. I fire off one shot, hitting them in the arm. Just as we collide, I pull a stake out of my pocket and swing.

We both go to the ground, and in the movement, my aim shifts and I embed the stake deep into the right side of the man's chest. He grabs both of my wrists, pinning them to the ground. With a beastly howl, he screams in my face, fangs fully extended.

I swing my knee up, catching him in the balls. Just as he's about to roll off of me in a fetal ball of pain, he's gone.

Rath flies through the air and the two of them tumble through the gravel. He locks his arm around the vampire's neck, choking him, as I scramble to my feet. Grabbing the other stake that fell from my pocket, I give a possessed war cry before jamming the stake through the vampire's rib cage and into his heart.

His body instantly grows gray and still. Rath lets him fall to the ground.

There on the back of his hand, is the branded symbol of the snake eating its tail.

I dig through his pockets and pull seven glass vials of green liquid out.

"He's looking for Born to take out," I say, my brows furrowing. "Did he know I'm a Born? That toxin won't work on me until I've resurrected."

Rath shakes his head and his eyes go to somewhere in the dark. He stands and walks with direction. I follow him.

My eyes adjust just as Lillian's shaking body comes into view.

"Lillian?" I breathe as I drop beside her. "What are you doing here?"

She's a mess. The needle is still embedded into her neck. A stake is poking out of her stomach, right below her rib cage. Claw marks trace down one of her arms.

I rip the needle from her neck. "Let's get her inside," I tell Rath.

He scoops her into his arms with no effort at all. I pull out my cell phone and call Ian as we walk into the house. It goes to his voicemail. "I know you're out looking for your own vamps, but I've got a dead one out on my front lawn if Bernie and Carl are feeling hungry tonight. Lillian just got attacked." I hang up.

Rath carries Lillian into the first guest bedroom on the ground floor. Gingerly, he lays her on the bed. Blood instantly stains the light blue comforter.

"Do you know why I have objected to your and Ian's relationship?" Rath asks with controlled anger in his voice.

I look back at him with a glare. This is so not the time.

"Because he makes you vulnerable," he says, his eyes hard and cold. "Feelings blind you in any relationship and getting involved with such a volatile enemy such as Mr. Ward is dangerous."

"Nothing about being in this town or this world will keep me safe from what is coming," I say as I look back down at Lillian. "Get over it."

Lillian's eyes are unfocused, but her lips move slightly, like she's trying to say something. I sit beside her on the bed and take her thin hand in mine.

"What can we do to help her?" I ask, once again feeling helpless. I look up at Rath.

"The toxin normally would take twelve hours to wear off," he says. Rath really is all knowing. "But with her injuries, it might take longer."

"Do I dare pull the stake out?" I ask in horror as I look back down at it. It's nearly fully saturated in blood. Had it just been three inches higher and to the left, it would have killed her.

"She'll live," Rath says. He stands stoic and removed. His hands folded in front of him.

"And there's no way to speed up the recovery process?" I ask in sadness. Lillian's eyes close in pain and she shakes harder.

Rath sighs, heavy and hard, like he doesn't want to divulge what he's about to tell me. "Blood not only sustains a vampire, it aids and quickens the healing process."

And when I glance back at Rath, he's gone. The bedroom door has been closed.

I look back down at Lillian and feel desperate. We aren't friends, but she is the one vampire who has been kind and understanding. She never wanted this life and she's shown sympathy over what is in store for me.

"What were you doing here?" I whisper as I push her short hair off of her forehead. She's sweating profusely. I need to get that stake out, but I'm scared to do it. I wish Ian were here. As an EMT, he deals with blood and gore all the time. It'd be no big deal to him.

Lillian clenches her teeth and breathes in hard, harsh pulls. And suddenly a scream rips from her chest.

I swear she's dying.

And I can't just sit here and watch.

"Lillian, nod if you can hear me," I say, feeling frantic. She takes a second, but she nods. "I've got to pull that stake out. You're not going to recover if I don't. I'm going to pull it out and then I need to be able to trust you."

I swallow hard. Because this is terrifying what I'm about to say.

"I'm going to trust you that you have damn good self-control," I continue. "You're going to feed on me, just enough to give you a boost. You will not kill me, you will not drain me. You hear?"

Her eyes open just a sliver. But I see commitment there. And gratitude. She nods her head.

"Okay," I say, trying to calm my thundering heart. "On three. One, two." But I don't wait till three. I yank the stake out on two.

She screams in pain, bunching up around her stomach. But I hold my arm out in front of her and shove it against her teeth.

And like a shot of adrenaline, her teeth latch into my skin.

It's been months since I've been bitten by a vampire, but I haven't forgotten what it feels like. The numbing sensation. The blurring out of my mind. The languid feeling of floating off into darkness. Lillian pulls the life from me, and I am both terrified and don't care.

I'm not positive how long it's been since she bit me, but eventually, she releases me. And instantly my brain starts to clear. I blink hard and my vision sharpens. My breathing returns to normal.

I look back down at Lillian. My blood is smeared all over her lips, clings to her teeth. But her face doesn't reflect agony any more. She looks in pain, but my eyes slide down and marvel.

Her skin is slowly knitting itself back together. The bleeding stops. The claw marks on her arm mend, leaving only crusted blood.

"Thank you," she manages to hiss. She's not out of the woods yet. Obviously, human blood doesn't reverse the effects of Elle's toxin or the House would have used that method. But she's recovering from her external physical injuries.

"You're welcome," I say, feeling slightly woozy. "How are you feeling?"

"Like piss, but it's better than shit," she gets out.

A tiny smile crosses my lips. Lillian is all class and beauty. It's odd hearing such vulgar words from her. I can only imagine what she's feeling right now.

"That is an improvement," I offer. "That was a pretty nasty attack."

"I should have been on guard," she says, angry with herself. "I know full well what's going on."

"What were you doing here, Lillian?" I ask, my brows furrowing. I take her hand in mine once again.

She looks up at me, her dark eyes serious and deep. "I came to warn you," she says. "I know you and Mr. Ward are involved. I saw you one night in town. You were trying to be careful, but sometimes a woman just knows."

I swear under my breath. "Does anyone else know about us?"

Lillian manages to shake her head. "I don't think so. But I thought you should know. Jasmine has given Micah permission to kill Ian."

All the blood in my body pools down to my feet. My fingers grow cold and stiff. My eyes freeze, wide and open.

Micah threatened Ian. He meant it. And Jasmine was just angry enough to let him do it. That was Ian's last straw that broke the House's back.

"You have to tell that boy to leave town," Lillian says. Her voice sounds far away. "It isn't safe for him in Silent Bend any more. Micah won't give this up until Ian's dead."

Twenty

LILLIAN SLEEPS. WHEN SHE'S SLEEPING, it's easy to forget that she's a vampire. An immortal Born. She just looks like a beautiful woman. Eyes closed, long lashes extending out over her beautiful brown cheeks. Hair a mess, but somehow still stylish. I wonder what she was like before she resurrected.

I watch over her as she sleeps for over an hour before the front door opens without a knock.

I don't respond when Ian calls out for me. I've sat and been terrified for him all night, let him worry over me for a few minutes. His booted steps sound up the stairs. Down to my bedroom. Around the upper floors. He comes back down. Checks the kitchen, the ballroom.

And finally he comes down the hall and sees me sitting on Lillian's bed through the open door.

He leans in the doorframe for a long time, arms crossed over his chest, not saying a word. I glare at him from under my lashes. Angry. Relieved. I'm a mixed bag of emotions right now.

"Nice work with the vamp outside," he finally says. His tone is trying to be light and joking, but there's knowledge of the reality behind it. He knows full well how unhappy I am. "Looks like it got you. You okay?"

He indicates my arm where Lillian fed on me. There's still dried blood smeared all over it.

"I'm fine," I say tersely. I don't want to tell him the truth about what I did, just to spite him.

"She'll be fine by evening, probably," Ian says awkwardly, indicating Lillian. He shifts his weight to both feet, pushing his hands into his pockets. "The toxin usually only lasts twelve hours."

"Yeah, I know that, Ian," I hiss. Carefully, I tuck the sheet up on Lillian's chest. I look her over one more time. Her eyes are narrowed, though they're shut. She still looks like she's in pain, even in sleep. Turning, I walk out behind Ian and close the door behind me.

We wander out and end up in the middle of the ballroom, standing on the family crest in the middle of the floor.

"What was she doing here?" Ian asks. He won't quite look me in the eye. He looks uncomfortable, nervous. He knows what he's done has pissed me off. And he has no idea how much worse it's gotten.

"She came here to warn me that Jasmine has given Micah permission to hunt you down and kill you." My words fall flat in the expanse of the marble ballroom.

Ian's eyes finally jump to mine. He bites the inside of his cheek.

He should look scared. He should be worried, at the very least. But his expression is just blank. And I hate him for not having a better sense of self-preservation.

"Did you hear me?" I hiss at him. "Micah, a vampire with a seriously bad attitude and muscles like you wouldn't believe is pissed at you and plans to kill you. The minute the sun goes down, he is going to be looking for you, and he will probably find you. And you are well trained and a bad ass, but there is a very good chance that he will kill you before you kill him. And even if you do kill him, then you'll have the entire House after you, wanting revenge. You will not survive this. Do you not understand, Ian? Don't you even care?"

There are tears in my eyes again and my throat is tight. I sound desperate, exactly how I feel inside.

"Of course I care, Liv," he says. He closes the distance between us and places his hands on my upper arms.

"Then why…" my voice is too emotional to continue.

"Because if I fight against them, maybe I can keep other kids from becoming orphans, too."

"Stop being so noble," I say, taking a step away from him. "You need to leave town. I will go to the House today and tell them they can take me now. That I'm ready to die *today*. It'll distract them. Hell, I'll tell Markov to kill me now and he'll be happy to do it in an instant just for sport. I'll resurrect, and they'll be so distracted by the King coming, they won't think twice about coming after you."

"Don't say those things, Liv," Ian says between clenched teeth as his eyes go wild and desperate. "You can't say those things because if you're willing to do all that, then you're breaking your promise."

I slap Ian. Hard. Right across the cheek.

"Don't you dare," I breathe, my breaths coming in hard and fast. "I am not in love with you and there's no way in hell you're in love with me or you would already be gone. So I guess this really is you keeping your promise, Ian."

"How can you say that, Liv?" Ian asks. His entire countenance is pained. His eyes, his expression, the downturn of his shoulders. "You've been there every day of the past three months that I have, too. I think you know damn well I was breaking that promise from the day you made me make it."

"Don't say that, Ian!" I scream. Tears are streaming down my face and I don't care. "You promised. We had an expiration and now, because of your choices, that date has been moved up to today. And you're not going to stop me."

I walk away from Ian right then. I take five steps before he pulls me to a stop.

"Alivia," Ian says as he grabs my wrist. "We will figure this out. I will find a way to stop this without running."

"You're so stupid," I whisper in anger as I turn back to him. The tears roll down my face freely. "Why'd you have to go and do... everything?"

"I never claimed to be a smart man." He takes a step toward me, closing the distance between us. He brings his free hand up to my face and touches his forehead to mine. "And I tend to do unexplainable things when it comes to you."

"Ian," I breathe as tears slip down my face.

Then his lips are on mine.

Our kiss is full of pain and fear. Our lips hover on each other, our mouths parted, breathing in all the weight of the situation and our lives. And then Ian's hand slides from my cheek to the back of my head and into my hair. His other hand slips around my waist and he closes the distance between us.

My body reacts without my permission, Ian has that power over me. One hand fists in his hair and the other clings to his chest.

We kiss like there's no tomorrow, which there isn't.

This is it.

This is the end of Ian and Alivia.

THE SUN IS ONLY SLIGHTLY warm on my back. It's mid-December, and while it's nothing like a Colorado winter, it's still winter here.

I lie with my head in Ian's lap. He traces his fingers down my back, sending currents of electricity racing through my veins. The blanket beneath me is growing slightly damp as we lie on it. But we're here, in this little world of no words and complete ignorance.

Because we're not talking. I can't say the words that need to be said, and Ian won't go like he should.

So we're here. Lying in front of the river. Touching. Kissing.

It's a final, bittersweet goodbye. Even if Ian won't admit it.

I roll over so that I'm looking up at him. Ian stares down at me, his eyes reflective of everything that's being cut so short. I reach up and place my hand on his cheek. It's rough. He hasn't shaved in a few days. The dark hair dots his face, darker than the wild hair on his head.

Ian really is a handsome man. Strong jaw, deep, hazel eyes. Hands that can kill and hands that can send goosebumps flashing across my skin with a feather-soft touch. Lips cut to the perfect shape. Those arms and that glorious chest.

I study him for a long time.

I'm going to miss this.

"Katina thought you all might be hungry." I sit up to see Beth walking out with a big silver tray. On it is a mix of cheeses, fruit, little sandwiches, and two glasses.

"Thank you," I offer. My voice sounds rough.

She sets it on the edge of the blanket. With a little nod of the head, she walks back into the house.

"That was thoughtful," Ian says. The first words we've spoken in an hour or more. Our make-out session made its way out here and neither of us has dared break the spell with reality. We're at an impasse.

"They're always taking such good care of me," I say, trying to smile and probably failing. "It's a small miracle that I don't weigh three hundred pounds after living off of Katina's cooking for the past four months."

"After being in the *South*," he corrects, trying to joke in that way he does. He takes a grape and pops it into his mouth. "We like our food deep fried and slathered in molasses and butter."

I take a sandwich and nibble off a bite. It's tasteless to me. This whole situation is awkward. This is unnatural and forced and we're just ignoring the immediate future.

"Yeah," I say, a good five beats too late.

"Do you like it here, though?" Ian asks. He finally meets my eyes and it's a genuine question. "Take out all the drama and the supernatural—do you like it here in Mississippi? Or do you wish you were still back in Colorado?"

I take another nibble and allow a few seconds to think about it. "Colorado is home. It's where I grew up. And it's a different world here, in so many ways. But…" It's difficult to put into words how I feel about Silent Bend. About the Conrath Estate. "I think this is where I was supposed to be, you know? Even though I didn't know Henry, he was my family and he's been here for more than two centuries. I have roots already planted here, I just didn't know it."

Ian reaches for a glass and takes a sip. I watch the glass come to his lips, watch the muscles constrict in his throat. He wipes the corner of his mouth with the back of his hand. "The South kind of has a way of gripping you and not letting go."

I nod, feeling my stomach sink. "Yeah, I can feel that."

Ian takes one more drink before setting his glass back on the tray. He leans forward and tips my chin back up, forcing me to look at him. "I'm glad you're here," he says, his voice low and intense. "Despite everything, I have no regrets."

He leans in and so do I. "I'm glad I'm here, too," I whisper just before our lips meet.

It's a tender kiss. One that lingers and sinks into my soul. It's a parting kiss and a last goodbye.

Because just five seconds into it, Ian collapses into my lap.

Tears spring into my eyes as I adjust him, laying him in my lap. I push the hair out of his face, tracing the back of my fingers along his rough cheek.

I told him I was glad I'm here, too, but I have many regrets.

Rath's footsteps sound softly over the grass. I don't look up at him, but I know it's him. He's always there.

"How long will he sleep for?" I ask.

"At least twelve hours," he answers in that soft, even tone of his.

I sniff hard and nod. I wipe a tear from the corner of my eye that's threatening to leak down my face. "And you'll give him another dose if this takes longer than that?"

"You have my word," Rath says.

Finally, I look up at him. His dark face is made even darker from his expression. There's a lot of hidden emotion behind those eyes. But he's here.

"Thank you."

Without another word, Rath bends and hoists Ian up over his shoulder. This shouldn't be an easy task; Ian is well built and has to be pushing six feet. But Rath gets him up with no strain and starts back for the house.

I feel sick as I follow him. This was my decision. I communicated what I needed from Rath with just a look across the room and he knew exactly what I needed. And now Ian is dangling from Rath's shoulders, mouth half open, dead to the world for the next half a day.

I did that to him.

But I had no other option.

Rath puts Ian in the room next to Lillian's. He lays him in the bed and gives me space to say goodbye. Rath goes back to the men working on a new, advanced lock system for this bedroom.

I stare down at Ian as he sleeps. A part of me wants to touch him. To take his hand. To put my lips on his cheek. To lie next to his side one last time.

But I can't. I want to remember our last moments together. As strained as they were, they were tender.

I don't know that I love Ian. There was never enough time to decide that, and I couldn't ever allow myself to sink that deep. But there's no denying it—Ian has forever changed my heart and being.

This is so painful.

"Goodbye," I whisper as one tear forces its way down my face.

I walk out of his room.

Rath waits for me in the foyer, beneath the chandelier. He stands there, hands always folded in front of him. His eyes follow me as I walk toward him.

"You are a brave soul, Alivia Ryan," Rath says. "You may not be a Conrath by name, but you are one by heart. Conraths make sacrifices for those they care about."

I blink a few times, clearing the moisture from my eyes. The time for tears is gone. "Yeah, well, it was going to happen in a few weeks, anyway. May as well get it over with."

In a move that surprises me, Rath closes the distance between us and wraps his arms around me. "I meant it when I said that I am always here for you. After you resurrect, I will come get you, and I will help you through this transition. The house will be prepared for you."

"Thank you," I say through my tight throat.

"Are you ready?"

I let go of Rath and turn to see Lillian standing behind us. She looks tired, but recovered. I just nod.

A minute later, we back out of the garage. I understand now why all of the windows are so heavily tinted. My father wanted to be able to go out at any time. Lillian does wear sunglasses, but she doesn't seem too bothered by the still shining light. It's nearly dusk.

Silently, I say goodbye to the daylight. Goodbye to the sun. Goodbye to swimming in the heat of the day. Goodbye to tanning. From here on out, the day is only going to cause me pain.

"If she won't kill me, you'll do it, right?" I say, trying to distract myself. "You'll do it right away if she won't agree to the plan?"

Lillian nods and pulls a gun from her purse. "Within the hour," she says.

I nod, gripping the steering wheel tighter. My knuckles are white.

I'd be so much less terrified about this situation if the resurrection process didn't take so long. I can go offer my death as a distraction, but once I'm dead, it will take four days before I'll rise again. I have to hope that Lillian and Rath will keep Ian safe during that time.

"Thank you again," Lillian says. "For your blood. For trusting me. I won't forget that."

I look over at her, and my chest suddenly swells with appreciation. I don't know that she's a friend, but she's the closest I've got in this demented town. "I know. And thank you for your help."

She reaches over and pats my leg. "You're a brave girl, Alivia. This is a terrible fate, for anyone. It isn't fair you're being forced into it before your time."

And the haunted tone of her voice, I wonder again. "How long have you been a vampire?"

Lillian sighs and looks out the window. "It's been twelve years," she says. "I grew up in Matal, just about an hour north of here. Terrible, little run-down town. I was into fashion and couldn't wait to get out of there. So I moved to New York as soon as I turned eighteen. I started making a name for myself. My designs were starting to catch fire. And then one day I was mugged. I was stupid, tried to fight back. The man shot me."

It's so easy to imagine, just like you see on those crime TV shows every night. Except the detectives didn't get the chance to solve her murder. I imagine her waking in a morgue and walking out of the building in complete confusion.

"I was older than you," she continues. "Forty-one and it still feels like my life was cut short."

"You didn't know you were a Born, did you?" I finally ask the question I've been suspecting for a while.

Lillian shakes her head. "I never knew my father. My mom said my dad died when I was little and I didn't ask too many questions."

"Vampires sure do like to sleep around, don't they?" I ask.

Lillian actually chuckles. "Well, when you've got eternity, you tend to get bored easily."

I shake my head. It's ridiculous.

But our light mood doesn't last long. We turn for the drive of the House and into the swamps. I remember Jasmine saying the land was cursed after Elijah's attack. I think I'd like to learn more about these curses. Maybe in four days.

The light begins to fade, but clings to the sky. I don't have much time until the sun goes down and Micah tries to take off to kill Ian. I very much doubt that he won't go ahead and do it now.

I park the Jeep right in front of the doors, as I did last time. The gravel squishes more than crunches when I get out. The ground is soggy and littered with moss and grass.

I would have knocked, but Lillian just opens the door and walks inside. This is her home, after all.

It's quiet inside. I wonder how many of the House members are still sleeping. How many hours of the day do they sleep when their preferred hours are so few? And do most of them sleep right as it gets light, or wake just as it gets dark?

We walk into the great room at the back of the house. It is laid out similarly to my own house, but this room is certainly not a ballroom. Instead, there's a giant, empty fireplace. Large enough that I could stand inside it and not bump my head. There's a TV stand set up in front of it, though. And several broken down couches surround it. Sitting on one, munching on a bowl of popcorn, is Cameron.

"Hey, princess," he says to me with a smile when he sees me. He stuffs another handful of popcorn into his mouth. "And I'm glad to see you, everyone's been worried about you." He indicates Lillian.

"Is Jasmine still sleeping?" Lillian asks. She doesn't use the same annoyance with Cameron that most everyone else in the House does. She's patient and grants actual respect to him. As if he really isn't the waste of space the rest of them treat him as.

"I don't think so," Cameron says, his eyes still on the TV. "Not with the racket going on in her bedroom. I think her and Micah have been *busy*, if you know what I mean."

Gross.

Someone bumps into me from behind, nearly sending me to the ground. Trinity walks past me and flops down onto the couch next to Cameron.

"Excuse you," I blurt in annoyance.

"Watch where you're standing." She glares at me with malice, even as she reaches for a handful of popcorn and starts in on it.

"Have some respect," Lillian chides Trinity. "You'll do well to remember that Alivia is royalty."

"She's also a human." But there's conflict in her voice when Trinity says this. Disgust, yes, but also a hint of longing. In their own ways, I suspect everyone here misses their human lives. Except probably Markov.

"Not for long."

Speak of the devil.

I turn to see Markov standing in the doorway. He wears trousers, his hands in his pockets, and a light blue button up shirt. He may be psychotic, but he's a well-dressed psycho.

"I need to speak to the House," I say to him. Because he feels the next highest ranked beside Jasmine, and I guess Micah. I also get the impression that he's one of the oldest vampires in the house and not just because he looks to be in his seventies. "I'm ready."

"Oh, my dear," he says with that scary smile of his. "No one is ever ready for this life."

"Probably not," I say. I try to subtly wipe the sweat of my palms on my pants. "But I'm tired of anticipating this. I want to get it over with."

My eyes flick behind Markov to see Jasmine walk down the stairs wearing a silk robe. Her hair is a wild mess that somehow still manages to look incredible. Micah follows behind her, wearing only a pair of boxers. The second he sees me, his eyes are filled with disdain.

"But there's still nearly three weeks until your birthday," Jasmine says. She steps into the room and I swear Cameron and Trinity both sit up straighter. "We agreed to not call the King until then."

I swallow hard. "I'm not talking about just calling the King. I'm talking about resurrecting. I want you to turn me. Tonight."

The countdown thunders inside my chest. The race to the finish.

The wheels are turning inside Jasmine's head. Once again, I've taken control of the situation from her hands. I'm turning the tables once more.

"I'm glad to see you are alright, Lillian," Jasmine says, changing the topic. "We began to fear the worst after you went missing for so long."

"I went for a walk to clear my head," she says. Not quite the truth, but I suppose it isn't a complete lie. "I was attacked. Thankfully, I wasn't far from Alivia's house and luck was with me I suppose because she found me. And killed my assailant."

"Another rouge Bitten?" Jasmine asks, tensing up.

I nod. "I didn't recognize him. I don't think it was anyone from town. But they had the same toxin as before and the brand on the back of his hand."

Jasmine mulls this over. This entire war from the dark has everyone reeling and not knowing what to do. "Thank you for taking care of one of our House members. That won't be forgotten."

As Markov told me once, proving loyalty in this House means far more than blood.

"Back to the reason I'm here," I say with a deep breath. "I want to do this. Now. And I am tired of anticipating this King coming and seeing if I am his queen, which I know I'm not. But I want him called here as soon as I've resurrected."

"Why are you in such a rush?" Jasmine asks, cocking her head to the side just a little.

"Because," I begin. I've been practicing the lie in my head since I made the decision to drug Ian. "Everything has been out of my control since I got here. I'm tired of it. This is me facing my fate and dealing with it."

For some reason, my eyes drift to Markov. He's wearing that terrible smile of his. But there's respect in his eyes and that surprises me.

"I think we should make it a grand affair," Lillian says. She embellishes my lie. "A ball at the House. Even though Alivia has said she does not wish to rule over us, we will be a part of each other's lives for many, many years to come, and we all hardly know each other. A House party, if you will. We could invite…guests."

And by this, she means people to feed on.

My stomach turns, knowing that very soon, this will appeal to me. I'll crave it. I'll enjoy it.

"When the time comes," I say, vocalizing the most terrifying part of my entire plan. But one I've very carefully thought out. "I want the entire House to take me. All nine of you. I want you all to feed on me until I'm dry and dead. It seems only fitting."

I feel the collective intake of breath and the anticipation that builds with it. For a moment, I'm afraid of what I've just suggested. Maybe it's offensive, or too extreme, even for a House of vampires.

"It's called a Bloodletting," Jasmine says. And when I look at her, she has a smile on her face. "It is the most honorable way to transition into a House. The ultimate act of acceptance, surrounding yourself to your House members. By letting them take from you. It is a legend among vampires and not often practiced because of the rarity of the situation that calls for it. I myself was transitioned this way."

The way she says it, like she's trying to undermine me, it makes my stomach boil.

I swallow hard once again and nod. Apparently, my morbid plotting isn't original. "That's the way I want it done."

A conflicted smile grows on Jasmine's face. "Very well. House members! We must get to work. We have a party to throw in an hour and a big finale just before dawn!"

Twenty-One

MY EYES FLICK TO THE clock once again. Three in the morning. I have three more hours until Ian starts to wake up. Until Rath will have to give him another dose. I have no doubts that Rath will give it to him, but Ian is Ian and his will is stronger than those around him most of the time.

There's the constant feeling on my shoulders that something *could* go wrong, so it *will*.

Voices collect downstairs. Laughter, talking, music. Even in the dead of night, a House of vampires are somehow able to concoct a party out of thin air.

I am the honored guest, here to die, and everyone else present to celebrate it.

"You look lovely," Lillian says as she puts the final touches on my hair.

I look in the full-length mirror in her room where we've been getting ready. A red dress, like blood, with spilling ruffles hugs my body. A corset top makes me look like a woman in all the right ways.

It's floor length. My hair is done up in an elegant twist and two white flowers are pinned into it.

I look like the princess everyone says I am.

"Thank you for all your help," I say quietly as my hands fidget.

"You are very welcome," Lillian says as she adjusts something with my hair. "And this doesn't leave this room, but I do wish you were fully claiming the House. You would make a fantastic ruler. You're smart, and crafty, and kind. And that's an uncommon combination."

I shake my head. "I hate politics. I know nothing about being a leader. I don't want it."

"Yet you've backed Jasmine into a corner, ripped the rug out from under her feet. You've gained my trust, made Markov doubt who should be in charge. Are you sure this isn't the life for you?" Lillian looks over my shoulder at me in the mirror.

"I want something I can't have." The words slip from my lips before I can think about them.

And the look in Lillian's eyes tells me that she knows exactly what I am talking about.

The door to Lillian's room opens and in steps Anna. "It's time. They're ready for you."

I turn and try to calm the fear that's threatening to claw its way up my throat.

Anna is severe-looking with her sharp cheekbones, intense eyes. Her hair is pulled back in a slick twist. A black leather corset top gives way to black tulle that falls to her knees.

She's fierce and beautiful at the same time.

The three of us walk out to the top of the stairs. Down below, the rest of the House members wait for us, accompanied by a dozen humans.

"Tonight we honor Alivia Ryan," Jasmine says, holding up a glass of red liquid, too thick to be wine. "With her sacrifice, our

House will be restored to honor, which it has not had for far too long. We thank you for your sacrifice."

"Here, here," they all say as they too hold up glasses. Cameron in a t-shirt mock-print tux. Trinity with a sneer. Micah with death in his eyes. The Kask brothers—Christian and Samuel—with hunger and lust. Markov with that curious look of anticipation. And Jasmine. It's difficult to read her.

I don't quite know what to do, so I take a little curtsey. And together, Anna, Lillian, and I, descend the stairs.

Samuel hands me a glass of wine as soon as I reach the bottom. "It helps if you're not stone cold sober when they do it," he says in a low voice. "Drink up."

I look up at him, surprised at his statement. I take the glass from him and down half of it. "Did you have a Bloodletting?" I ask.

Samuel shakes his head. "Our father used to rule the house before Jasmine. He was a friend of Elijah Conrath's, had been for a long time. So when Elijah was killed, my father took over. He wanted to grow the House, so he slept around, a lot. Christian and I were the only ones to take. But he always planned to kill us when we reached our prime. We knew it was coming."

"That's awful," I say, shaking my head. And I down the rest of my drink.

"Dying's not so bad," he says with a flirtatious smile. "It's the resurrecting part that's a bitch."

I want to demand he explain what he means by that, but he walks off. The party is making its way throughout the House.

"He's right," someone whispers into my ear. I turn to see Christian leaning in close. "The resurrection isn't all that pleasant, but it's a small second in the grand scheme of an immortal life."

I swallow hard. As if I wasn't nervous enough before. "How long have you been a vampire?" I ask instead of looking scared and weak.

"I'm about to hit my sixty-seventh anniversary," he says with a smile. "Forever twenty-six. My brother forever twenty-four."

"How did your father die?" I ask. I try not to look at Trinity biting into the neck of a teenage boy in the corner of the room. Or the blood that drips to the floor. Or the glazed-over look in his eyes.

"There's a reason everyone is afraid of the King," Christian says as his voice grows darker. "Cyrus came for a visit fifteen years ago. I think he was investigating why we no longer had a Royal. I guess in his multiple millennia lifespan, two hundred years wasn't so long to get around to it. He'd gone to see Henry, who acted very Henry. Cyrus was mildly annoyed. And so he called a game. If my father could defend himself against two dozen humans—armed humans— the King would instate my father as a fully fledged Royal."

"He didn't survive," I fill in when Christian falters in his story.

He shakes his head. "The King shamed my brother and I. Said our family's blood had grown weak. That we didn't deserve leadership of the House. Jasmine took over a week later."

This House should be mine, but in a way, it should also be Christian or Samuel's. But there are deep politics in this world, and the demented King controls all.

No wonder everyone is so afraid of him coming here.

"This world is messed up," I say as a human pours me more wine.

And I mentally slap myself for the thought. I'm already separating myself from my own species. She's just a person. I'm a human, too.

For the next hour.

A woman walks up to Christian, her hands all over him. She leans in seductively, whispering in his ear. A coy smile forms on his lips. "You'll have to excuse me. Bianca here has needs I must attend to."

"You're disgusting." Anna walks up and Christian smiles at her as Bianca leads them away.

"They're both man whores," Anna says with a shake of her head. "Don't let their charms fool you." And the way she says it, I suspect there's history between her and one of the brothers, maybe even both.

"Samuel has already tried and failed," I say, remembering the Summer Ball. "Trust me, neither of them holds any attraction to me."

"Good," she says with disgust in her voice.

"Can you explain something to me?" I ask as I watch Christian disappear through a door. Cameron is watching Trinity, even as he sinks his fangs into a woman's neck.

"Of course," Anna responds.

"These people are here willingly," I say. "They even seem to be enjoying what's going on. The House appears to have a constant rotation of Bitten. There's a connection there, isn't there?"

Anna nods. "Jasmine has the entire house recruit 'feeders.' People who are willing to be fed upon at any time they're called. We only recruit a few people from Silent Bend, otherwise we cause too much of a stir. Some are from surrounding towns, one or two are even from across the river. But they let us feed on them in exchange for the promise that one day we will turn them."

"They want to become a Bitten?" I ask in disbelief.

"Humans have long had a fascination with the supernatural," she continues to explain. "Anything beyond what is their mundane lives. Each of these people here are willing to trade possibly years of servitude in exchange for what little benefits being a Bitten gives them."

"I've heard about the Debt," I say as I watch one of the very Bitten we speak of pour Lillian a glass of red liquid.

"Jasmine enforces it with every ounce of strength she possesses." Anna takes a sip of blood from her glass. "Let us feed on you for however long we deem necessary. We drain you of enough blood to turn you. Serve your term with the Debt. And go free as a Bitten into the world."

I shake my head. "I don't understand the Bitten. They just accept their servitude."

"I understand civil war," Anna says. And I don't doubt what she says. "There will come a day when the vampires will have their own."

"How long have you been part of the House?" I ask. I watch Jasmine and Micah dance, spinning in carefree circles. He dips her, kissing between her breasts as her head falls back, and she laughs.

"Only five years," she responds. She crosses her arms over her chest and settles her weight onto one foot. It's strange, she's incredibly beautiful, maybe the most beautiful woman in the House, but she's sharp, tough, and has a piss-off attitude that's far more mature than Trinity's. "I used to be a rouge. A wanderer without any ties. But it's a lonely life."

"You prefer this life over freedom?" I ask, surprised.

"It's not like that," she says with the shake of her head. "It's about being with others like you. Who understand you. I have a theory that you'll only keep yourself separate from us for a few years at most. I don't know how your father stood it for all those years."

I hadn't considered it before. Will this life eventually get lonely? It's makes sense. Being only able to go out at night, and everyone in this town is afraid of the dark. Who will I talk to? Rath? He's the only guarantee of who will stay in my life. I'll loose Ian. Elle. Even Daphne and Fred.

But the House will be here, and they will understand everything I will be going through.

No. I won't ally myself with Jasmine. Ever.

"How long has it been since you resurrected?" I ask, changing the conversation.

"I was killed in the Revolutionary War," Anna says. Her eyes grow dark and distant. "I pretended to be a boy so I could join the fight. I lasted four months before someone ran me through with a bayonet."

It's astounding. She's told a huge, incredible story in just three short sentences. Mentally, I try to calculate just how old she is. Two hundred and fifty something years.

"I'm the oldest in the house," she continues. "Next is Markov. He's about to hit his two hundred year mark in the spring. Then Jasmine. She's 125. Then the Kask brothers. Trinity, then Micah, Lillian, and baby Cameron. He's only seven years post-resurrection."

Between all of the house members there is so much history. The things they've seen. The wars they've lived through. The revolutions and the changes. It's incredible.

And all of that potential for such a profoundly long life is laid before me.

I'm supposed to be at work right now. I should be working side by side with Fred, getting the pastries for the day ready. But I'll never set foot in that heaven-scented shop again.

The party carries on. I'm anxious the entire time, and I try not to let it show. But then again, my sweating palms, increased heart rate, my anxiety that I know every one of them can sense is totally justified. They just don't know the real source it originates from.

When the time nears five a.m. and the sun will soon start creeping up in the horizon, things begin to wind down. Half a dozen humans are passed out on the floor in random places. Others sit, in a blood-drained haze. I don't know where the rest are. I hope they're alive. I wonder if any new Bitten have been created tonight.

But the House members all look happily satisfied. Full of blood. Knowing they are soon to be returned to honor.

"It's time," Jasmine says. She comes up from behind me and lays a hand on my shoulder.

My heart both flutters out of control and calms, if that's even possible. *It's time.*

I remember that all these vampires have perfect, enhanced hearing because Jasmine didn't say it very loud, yet every one of them comes from one part of the house or another.

"I thought we could have a beautiful goodbye to your old life," Jasmine says as we start walking toward the front door. "I thought we could do the Bloodletting outside, where you can see the sun begin to rise. But, having been converted to your new life, you'll die just before the sun rises."

How morbid. "Alright," I say instead.

Death.

I'm going to die.

Right now.

One of the Bitten opens the doors wide.

The sun is only faintly starting to lighten the horizon. A pale haze of gray-green on the horizon. I squint against the dark, even as I hear Lillian give a sharp intake of breath. Micah hisses, a low, throaty thing. One step. Two steps. Down I walk, toward my fate.

As I reach the bottom step, the world falls away.

There's a figure, sitting and bound to a chair. Unconscious.

It's Ian. Sitting before the very House I am here to protect him from.

"What's going on?" I manage to get out. It's a muttered, strangled thing.

"Mr. Ward here has annoyed the House for the last time," Jasmine says as she walks down and stands behind Ian. She traces her hand along one of his shoulders, drags it behind his head and over the other shoulder as she walks around him. "He's a nuisance to us all. We've been wanting to be rid of him for a year or so now, but he's a tricky one to catch. Last night, I tasked Bronson here in tracking him down."

"What are you going to do with him?" My voice is little more than a whisper.

"He's a gift," Jasmine says. She looks up at me from beneath her falsely long lashes. "For you. Once you resurrect, you will be thirsty in a way you can't imagine. Your first feed is always a draining one. And since you had him drugged and in captivity in your own home, I thought you might want to do the honors."

I'm pretty sure there's no way my heart is beating anymore. My chest is an empty, hollow thing. There's already no more blood in my body and surely I am dead already.

Maybe this is all just a nightmare.

But there's Ian. With his head slumped to one side. His mouth hangs open just slightly. His body is entirely limp. The only reason he hasn't collapsed to the ground is the cords that bind him to the chair.

"No," I breathe. I shake my head. There aren't words for the turn this evening—morning—has taken.

"No," Jasmine says. Even as she does, I feel the crowd around me tighten. "What do you mean no? Surely he must have done something to you to warrant you drugging him and locking him up."

Rath.

What happened to him? How did a simple Bitten get past Rath? What have I done?

"This is a gift, Alivia," Jasmine says. Her eyes grow dangerous and dark. She walks slowly toward me. Micah's hand suddenly clamps down around my wrist. Trinity grabs my other. Instinctively, I fight against them. "We could have made you go into town and hunt down your own first meal like an animal. But here we are, offering you a gift, like the royalty that you are. You should be thanking us. Unless there's a reason you object to the specific meal?"

And there's a beat. In my chest. In my ears. In my throat. Throughout my entire body.

"I can't," I say. My voice is barely heard. "Not him."

"Why not?" Jasmine asks. Her own voice grows lower and quieter with each syllable. And a red glow ignites in her eyes.

"Not him," I breathe, shaking my head.

I feel Lillian's hand on my shoulder from behind. It tells me not to say a word. That revealing the truth will only make things worse.

But I can't.

"She loves him." It's Markov. His voice is thoughtful. Slightly amused. But there's a hint of reverence in it.

Everyone is silent as Jasmine walks up to me. I feel her eyes burning into me. She'd kill me now if she knew I wouldn't resurrect. But I don't look at her. I simply stare at Ian.

I did this. If I hadn't drugged him, he would have easily fought that Bitten off. He would have killed him. Ian wouldn't be here right now. And I wouldn't be asked to kill him.

All my organs turn to lead as Ian's eyes flutter open.

No! I internally beg. *Don't wake up. Please don't witness this. Please, no!*

Jasmine still stares at me, but I can only watch in horror as Ian struggles to clear the fog from his head.

Slowly, he lifts it. His eyes are squeezed closed for a moment. He stretches his neck from one side to the other. A low groan makes its way from his chest.

And every pair of vampire eyes snaps to him.

"Holy shit," Ian breathes when he finally opens his eyes. He takes everyone in, blinking rapidly as if to make what he's seeing fade into a dream. His eyes land on me last. They grow in terror. "Liv," he breathes. "Liv, don't do this! Please, don't do this!"

My throat tightens. Tears once again spring into my eyes.

I've ruined everything.

"Liv," Ian whispers. I see moisture gleaming in his own eyes.

"I'm sorry," I say. But I doubt he can hear it.

Cameron suddenly gives a choked off cry and crumples to the ground. A tiny needle sticks out of his neck.

I hear a tiny whistling sound and then Micah goes down, as well.

"Enough!" Jasmine screams like a maddened woman. I watch in horror as she draws a long-blade knife from the folds of her dress.

"No!" I scream, trying to jerk out of Trinity's hold. But she's yanked both of my arms behind my back. Her sharp fingernails dig into my skin, but I don't feel it.

Moving faster than I can see, Jasmine is standing before Ian. She leans in close, whispers something into his ear.

I think Ian mutters something. But it's cut off.

Jasmine shoves the knife up through Ian's stomach, the length of it disappearing inside him.

A demented scream rips its way from my body. Except I feel nothing. Only the sharp sting of the blade I cannot see. I jerk against Trinity's hold and everything slows.

I see every millimeter of steel as it slides out of Ian's body. Blood gushes from the wound. Ian's face. His face... It's frozen. Not in terror. Not in pain. Simply in shock and disbelief. His eyes stare at Jasmine. He blinks. Slow. So slow. And when he opens his eyes again, he's looking right at me.

I think it's his name that is pouring from my lungs into the lightening morning.

And suddenly I'm free. My feet are flying down the final step, across the gravel. There's a flash beside me, and I think it's Lillian who rips the ropes from Ian's body and flies at Jasmine.

But all I can process is catching Ian's falling form as he collapses out of the chair. I'm soaked in his blood when his torso crashes into mine and we both go down into the gravel.

"Ian, Ian," I'm whispering, over and over. I press my hands into his bleeding, gushing wound. There's so much blood. Just pouring out of him like a river.

"Li...Liv," he manages to get out in a breath. Blood bubbles up in his mouth, staining his teeth and lips. His hand shakes as he raises it up to my face.

Blood smears over my cheek as he brushes his thumb over it. "Tell me what to do," I finally manage a coherent thought. "You could save you. Tell me what to do."

He tries to say something. But he's drowning in his own blood. So much blood.

"Ian," I call desperately. His hand falls away from my face. "Ian!" I press my hands harder into the wound with one hand and try to sit him up with my other. If I could just clear the blood from his throat. If I could just make it easier for him to breathe.

But I'm sitting in a pool of Ian's blood. And it's leaking from his mouth. And he takes a gurgled breath.

"Ian," I whisper.

And his body goes limp.

"Ian?"

My hands shake. Realizing that there's no more breath being pulled into his body, I pull my hands back. My mouth hangs open, not pulling in any air, either.

The sound of a body dropping behind me pulls me back into reality. And I jump when the growl of a motorcycle rips through the morning.

I turn to take in the scene. Micah, Cameron, and Samuel all lie on the ground, immobile. The rest of the House members cower in a semi-circle, retreating into the house.

"Get on."

My eyes dart up when the motorcycle comes to a screeching halt beside me. Rath extends a hand down and grips my forearm. "Get on."

He doesn't wait for me to react. He hauls me onto it. "But Ian!" I scream as he starts to drive away.

"He's dead," Rath says as he wraps one of my arms around his waist. "There's nothing you can do for him now."

I look back toward Ian as we start speeding down the driveway. Instead, I see Jasmine, darting after us.

Like he knew exactly where she was, Rath turns in his seat, gun extended, and shoots. He catches her in the chest, on the right side, and she goes down. Rath guns the gas, and we rip through the pale light.

We're nearly back to the Estate before I realize that Rath is covered in blood. And it isn't just Ian's blood—*Ian's blood*—transferring from me to him. Rath is bleeding everywhere.

The gates to the Estate swing open as it comes into view. Gravel spits everywhere as we race up the drive. We pull straight into the garage and it shuts behind us.

"Come on," Rath says in the dim light. "Let's get you cleaned up."

He has to help me off of the motorcycle. I'm a frozen, in shock statue. And my dress is tangled around me. Everywhere. Rath places one hand under my elbow, the other on my waist and half drags me off of the bike. With stiff, shuffling steps, we walk into the house.

Two of the staff members wait for us in the kitchen. They stand there, hands folded in front of them, at attention.

"Draw Miss Ryan a bath," Rath instructs the woman. She darts off without hesitation. Rath turns to Antonio. "You lock down the house. No one comes in tonight. No matter what."

The man nods and heads off.

"Come on," Rath says. He's still holding onto me and it's only now that I realize how much of my weight he is supporting. He winces as we try to make our way toward the stairs.

As we round the corner into the foyer, I see the dead body lying in the middle of the floor. When we get closer, I see it's one of the gardeners. Juan.

There's a knife embedded into his back.

Somehow still possible, my face blanches all the more.

But I don't ask. My brain can't process more. More death. More blood. More everything. I concentrate on taking the stairs one at a time.

Rath guides me into the bathroom where the water is running and the water is frothing with bubbles. When I simply stand there, numb and empty, Rath instructs Angelica to help me undress and get into the water.

Most of the blood was soaked into my dress, but a healthy amount covers my arms, my chest, and my face, so the water of the bath instantly turns a shade of pink.

It's a literal bloodbath.

When the water is full, the woman shuts it off and exits the room. I hear Rath muttering quietly to her, but the words don't process in my brain.

Rath limps into the room. I see the nasty gash in his leg. Wide and gaping. But not bleeding like it probably should. There's another gash down his opposite arm, and claw marks down one side of his face.

He's a wreck.

"Are you ready?" he asks as he sits on the divan. The bathroom is idiotically large enough to accommodate it.

For the first time, I meet his eyes. They're deep and dark. They're prepared and calm. Same as always.

Dependable, loyal Rath.

I'm so lucky to have him. Just as my father was.

I swallow, and nod.

Because I have to be. I have to not drown. I have to know how the events of the night happened.

"I was in the library," Rath says. He rubs his dark hands together, but doesn't look at them. I think they are itching for action.

"Listing what would need to be done to the house to prepare for your resurrection. It was an hour until I needed to give Ian his next dose and I planned to give it to him in thirty minutes. Juan came in, which should have tipped me off. The garden staff have no business being in the house in the middle of the night. But he's worked for the family for years with not a sign of betrayal. He said he needed to talk to me."

My eyes fall to the injury on Rath's leg.

"He pulled a blade on me before I could react. He caught me off guard, and I'm ashamed of that," he looks away from me.

I should comfort him. Tell him that there was no way he could know. That he should be able to trust his own staff. But I'm too angry. Too full of everything, that if I open the doors, it all with come pouring out of me and then there will be nothing left but an empty skin bag full of bones.

"I went down and couldn't even fight him off—or the Bitten that Juan then let in through the damn front door. The Bitten grabbed Ian from his room and was out the door in less than ten seconds. But Juan can't move as fast as a vampire."

I imagine the scene. Rath on the floor of the library, bleeding out. But grabbing a knife from somewhere on his person, I have little doubt, and embedding it in Juan's back. Ending his life right then.

"I failed this family," Rath says in a cool and even voice. His eyes fall to the marble floor. "And for that, I am truly sorry."

Rath is strong. He's a rock. He doesn't make mistakes.

So seeing him, *him* like this. It's what finally breaks me.

I reach over, take his hand in mine. And let the tears consume me.

Twenty-Two

DURING THE BRIGHTEST LIGHT OF the next day, Rath goes with Elle to collect Ian's body. I ask him to go, and he does with shame in his eyes.

No police will be called. There will be no murder investigation. There will be no trial and no prison time.

There will only be a devastated grandmother and little sister. There will only be a body in a box and a hole in the ground.

It all happens very quickly, and I can only figure it is with Rath's taking control. A burial plot is arranged, right next to George and Cora Ward's headstones. The following morning, a hearse drives Ian's body to the grave.

I lock everything up. I put my pain in a box and hide it in the darkness of my soul. It won't be let out until the time is right. But right now, I simply need strength. I stand beside Elle, holding her hand. Lula stands on the other side of her. She mutters things under her breath every once in a while, shaking her head. About every two minutes, she shoots a dark glare in my direction.

A pastor gives a generic sermon on life after death and God's plan. There's no hint of Ian in it. It could apply to any John Doe.

Rath watches us all from the shadows. I don't see him, but I can feel him there. Ready. He's injured, but I'd still bet on him in any fight. He won't be caught off guard again.

There are no other attendants of Ian Ward's funeral.

There's a stone in my stomach that grows heavier and heavier as they lower Ian's casket into the earth. He's all on his own down there and that wet, dark dirt looks so cold.

Silent tears work their way down Elle's face. She leans her head on my shoulder and I hold her as she silently weeps.

Neither of us speaks a single word through the entire service. It's short. And cold. Just like Ian's end was.

I go back to Lula's house. I want to be with Elle. She needs a sister or a mother in this situation, and since she has neither, I want to be a stand in. But I only last thirty minutes before Lula cusses me out of the house.

I wander slowly across the backyard that leads to the cabin. The stairs creek loudly as I walk up them. It starts to rain lightly when my fingers touch the doorknob. For a moment, I rest my forehead on the door, close my eyes, and pretend.

Ian is on the other side of that door. He's sitting on the couch, sharpening a knife as he watches some old school action movie. When I walk through the door, he'll look at me. That lopsided smile will pull on one side of his mouth. His eyes will unabashedly run me up and down. I settle down into his lap and he'll kiss me and make promises he has no intension of keeping.

I take a deep breath, and twist the doorknob.

The cabin is cold. The fireplace in the corner is dark. There's a few dirty dishes in the sink. Ian's bed is unmade. There's a bag on the table that's full of weapons. The remote sits innocently on the couch.

It's like the cabin is just waiting for him to walk back through the doors.

And that's not going to happen.

The floor creaks under my feet as I cross through the kitchen and into Ian's bedroom. Springs push back at me when I lie on the bed. And Ian's scent envelops me as I rest my head on his pillow.

Anger is what keeps my heart from breaking into a thousand sharp shards as I stare up at the ceiling.

THE RAIN HASN'T LET UP as I stare down at the freshly turned dirt. My jacket has long since soaked through. Rath knew better than to offer the umbrella he holds in his hand. He stands back at a distance.

Even when footsteps come up from the side. I don't turn when someone stops beside me and observes the grave as well.

Jasmine doesn't say anything for a long time. The mix of emotions roll off of her like a tangible cloud. I wonder if she really was bi-polar in her human life. I'm not sure if she's more extreme now or if she was completely out of control before.

"I know you're angry with me now," she finally says. "But eventually you'll realize that I did us all a favor. You'll return to the House. And we'll finish what we started."

My jaw clenches hard. Hard enough to threaten to crack my teeth.

"You may not be ready by your birthday anymore," Jasmine says. "But it won't be long."

And the tone of her voice tells me that she will make me ready whether I am or not.

"You have a fatal flaw," I say evenly.

"Enlighten me," she challenges.

"You believe that people will do what you say, simply because you place yourself upon a throne." My fingers ball into a fist. Air flows into my lungs in deep pulls. The anger and the hatred that has been building up inside of me for so long now comes out in eerily calm confidence. "That they will remain loyal to you because you tell them they should."

"I've made sacrifices for the House," Jasmine says, her voice dipping. The desperation surfaces in her tone. "I have kept it running for a decade and a half because your father chose to abandon us."

A smile forms on my lips. I let my eyes slide closed and shake my head. She truly doesn't get it.

I take another deep breath. Give myself two seconds to collect. When I open my eyes, I turn to face her. I take two steps toward her, so we are only a foot apart.

"You've taken and taken," I say, completely calm and collected. "And now, I promise that I will take from you what you love most."

There's a moment of reflection as Jasmine tries to figure out what she loves most, which tells me that she is incapable of the true meaning of the word.

"You'll never take Micah from me," she scoffs from behind her dark sunglasses. "He hates you far more than I do. He'll kill you before you get within fifty feet of him."

Again, the smile pulls on the corners of my lips. "Keep your man toy. I vow to take what you love most, and that, Jasmine Veltora, is the House. I will disassemble it right from under your feet and watch you fall. Alone. The Conrath family hasn't claimed the House for two hundred years, but that's about to change. The House is mine. And I'm taking it."

Jasmine's eyes slowly grow wide, her mouth falling just slightly open.

Without a breath from her, I turn, and walk back to the car.

Twenty-Three

WHEN YOU TAKE AWAY HOPE, free spirit, the possibility of new love, and all the things that make life bright and worth living, all you're left with is revenge and anger.

I pace in front of the chalkboard in my father's office. On it, I've written the names of each member of the house.

I'm pretty sure I've already won Lillian. I haven't seen her since the night of my party, but I imagine she's keeping herself safe. Lying in wait until I make a move. There's nothing she can do for now.

I think I can win Anna over. She doesn't seem particularly loyal to anyone in the house. It's companionship she craves. And a strong backbone. She doesn't seem to dislike me by any means. I will figure out how to sway her to my side.

The Kask brothers. I'm not sure how they will play out. Samuel flirts endlessly, but flirtation means nothing. Christian is always known to smile at anything with breasts. But Christian told me that story of his father and how he was the leader before Jasmine. I think I can use that information to my advantage.

I will never want Micah in my house. He had a line drawn through his name the second I wrote it up there.

I doubt that I will be able to gain the allegiance of Trinity, either. I don't know why she doesn't like me, but somehow I feel that isn't going to change.

Cameron will be easy, I think. Be his friend, give him a smile when he cracks a joke, provide him with plenty of salty snacks, and he'll be anyone's best friend.

It comes down to Markov. If I can gain him, I know I can do this. With his support, the others won't question me. He has that kind of power, which makes me wonder why he isn't the leader instead of Jasmine. Then again, he is driven by his lust for blood. It's hard to lead when you're constantly thinking about your next kill.

He will be the most complicated one to win over.

"Revenge is a dangerous game."

I turn to see Rath standing in my doorway. Hands clasped behind his back. Expression calm and even.

"This isn't just a game of revenge," I say as I face my board again. "It's a game of power."

"And that was the downfall of many royals throughout all history," he says.

I take a deep breath, feeling it rattle my core. I've grieved. I still grieve. I've lost Ian. He was killed because of me. And that could destroy me. Could rip my soul to pieces. Could render me useless in my bed for months to come. But instead I choose to channel it. "I can't just do nothing. Someone has to change this madness."

"And that I understand." I hear Rath's boots cross into the room. I look back to see him place something on the desk.

It's a crown. Golden and ornate. It holds but a single red jewel in its center, right above the relief of a crow, it's wings widespread, stretching along the length of it.

"But I beg you to play carefully."

I set the stick of chalk down on the tray and cross to the desk. Cautiously, hesitantly, my fingers trace over the cold metal. I pick it up and study it's intricacies.

A vampire crown for a vampire royal. The word has always felt like an unreal thing. Something that's said, but holds no real meaning.

But seeing this crown, touching it, feeling it's solid weight, the meaning behind that word begins to take reality.

I am a *royal*. A Born vampire princess. I am the descendent of a literal King.

"The crown has been in your family line for over eight hundred years, since the inception of the Conrath name. The House of Ravens. Honor the name well as you play this dangerous game."

Both our eyes jump to the door when there's a single heavy knock from the front door. It's followed by just one more.

My mind races through all the possibilities of who it could be. Elle. Lillian. Jasmine. It's dark outside. So really, it could be any of the House.

Rath takes a step toward the door, but I hold a hand out. "No," I say. He looks back at me with uncertainty. "I'll go."

His eyes argue with me.

I shake my head as I set the crown back on the desk. "I'm done being afraid. A ruler isn't afraid. And it's time to rise."

Rath takes a step back, clearing the doorway for me, and bows his head in consent.

I walk past him, but feel his presence not far behind. My bare feet pad over the cold, polished marble floor. The chandelier hangs above me, like a floating crown to mark this ancient and grand house.

Anticipation makes my palms slick. My fingers close around the knob. I take one deep breath, readying myself for whoever might be behind the door. My other hand wraps around a stake.

The door doesn't even creak when I pull it open.

Black veins sprout from around glowing, tired, yet wild red eyes. He leans with one hand on the doorframe, the other pushing absentmindedly against the door. His mouth hangs open slightly, as if in a daze. Extended fangs gleam in the light.

"Ian." The word escapes me in a whisper that won't return to my chest.

"Liv," he breathes, rough and wild. "I'm so damn thirsty."

THE END OF BOOK ONE

ACKWNOLEDGEMENTS

This book was written because my fans have continued to support me for the last five years. Five years! You've stuck with me and you still like to ready my crazy stories. Thank you, so much for still being there by my side!

Thank you to my beta readers: Jenni, Janett, Brittany, and Lauren! Thank you so my editor Sarah. It really takes a team to make a book worthy of going out in public.

Thank you to my family. You're always there for me, cheering my crazy side on. And thank you to my Father above.

ABOUT KEARY

 Keary Taylor grew up along the foothills of the Rocky Mountains where she started creating imaginary worlds and daring characters who always fell in love. She now splits her time between a tiny island in the Pacific Northwest and Utah, dragging along her husband and their two young children. She continues to have an overactive imagination that frequently keeps her up at night.

To learn more about Keary and her writing process, please visit www.KearyTaylor.com.

CPSIA information can be obtained
at www.ICGtesting.com
Printed in the USA
BVOW04s0344100317
478299BV00001B/24/P